Mary A. Morton

Abbie Saunders

A Story of Pioneer Days in Minnesota

Mary A. Morton

Abbie Saunders
A Story of Pioneer Days in Minnesota

ISBN/EAN: 9783744747370

Printed in Europe, USA, Canada, Australia, Japan

Cover: Foto ©Andreas Hilbeck / pixelio.de

More available books at **www.hansebooks.com**

ABBIE SAUNDERS.

— A —

Story of Pioneer Days

IN MINNESOTA.

By MARY A. MORTON.

FRESNO, CAL.
PUBLISHED FOR THE AUTHOR.
1892.

DEDICATION.

TO

My Dear Aunt,

WHOSE KIND INTEREST GREATLY ENCOURAGED THE
WRITING OF THESE PAGES, IS THIS BOOK
RESPECTFULLY DEDICATED BY

The Author.

PREFACE.

In this age of the world, when, as it were, a flood of trashy literature is sweeping over the land, developing the habit of reading without thought, and putting fantastic ideas of life, which are as untrue as they are unreal, into the minds of the young, it would be out of place to make any apology for the present effort to aid in stemming this tide of evil.

There are many ways in which this good work might be accomplished. Among these might be mentioned the precept and example of those who are in authority over the young, or are held in high esteem by them. A word from such explaining the nature of trashy reading, and its effect upon the mind, from a physical standpoint, will often have the effect of causing young people to take heed to their course before they have gone too far, thereby becoming unable to concentrate their minds upon any other than that which is light and trifling. When such precept is coupled with example in the same direction, it will have a still more beneficial effect.

But the young must have something to read which is pleasing, and, therefore, not a task. The most common excuse for indulging in romance is that there must be some relaxation from study. This is true. The physical system requires change of occupation, so, also, does the mental organism. This change must be something into which the individual will enter with zest, or no good will be accomplished. If there is nothing better provided for such an emergency, the inevitable result will be that recourse will be had to that which is degenerating in its nature. How important it is, therefore, that, in keeping the mind in the right channel, books at once true to life and deeply interesting should be placed before the reading public.

While authors should not ignore the thrilling incidents of real life, of which there are many in every person's experience, still they should not make such the predominating feature of the tale. In the following pages the story of Abbie Saunders is told in a highly interesting style, and with careful regard for exact truth, the names only being fictitious. The old adage that "truth is often stranger than fiction," is strongly exemplified in these chapters. Although the sequence of events and style of narrative are such as to create a deep interest at the very beginning, and hold the same to the close, the tendency of the story is to nerve the reader to greater earnestness in the duties of every-day life, instead of unfitting him for those duties.

The thread of Christian experience is woven in so naturally as to cause the reader involuntarily to desire the same experience. While this is not made so prominent as to repel unbelievers, yet it is impossible to read the narrative without perceiving that the sustaining power which was with Miss Saunders emanated from the throne of grace. This is the strongest impression left upon the reader in finishing the book. From this reason, if from no other, Christians should aid in its circulation.   A. J. MORTON.

CONTENTS.

Chapter.		Page.
I.	Childhood Days	11
II.	Incidents of Girlhood Days	16
III.	Charley Reynolds	35
IV.	The Family Move West	43
V.	The Wedding	55
VI.	Darker Days	69
VII.	The Birth of Little Ella	76
VIII.	Further Cruelties	91
IX.	Abbie Rescued from Danger	102
X.	Rushford's Departure and Return	114
XI.	The Trial	129
XII.	Arrest and Trial for Divorce	141
XIII.	Rushford Escapes and Appears as a Ghost	148
XIV.	Further Annoyances from Rushford	170
XV.	Abbie Visits Her Brother	185
XVI.	Rushford's Plots	193
XVII.	Executing His Plot	204
XVIII.	Rushford Kidnaps the Child	222
XIX.	The Flight	234
XX.	Jim Brooks' Story	249
XXI.	Recovery of the Child	270
XXII.	The Case Finally Decided in Abbie's Favor	284

ABBIE SAUNDERS.

CHAPTER I.

CHILDHOOD DAYS.

O N the broad prairies of Illinois, some twenty miles from Galena, might be seen, at the time our story opens, a farmhouse, standing on a small eminence, and overlooking a meadow, beyond which flowed the small stream known as Muddy Branch. This stream was the boundary line on one side of some two hundred acres of land, which we will call Olney farm. Its present owner, Mr. Saunders, had started, some seven years before, from the State of Michigan, to find a home on the famed prairies of Illinois. He brought with him his wife and four small children.

After much weary traveling, he arrived in Galena, and was obliged to stop there, as winter was coming on. Here was born the heroine of our story, who was called Abigail. The names of the older ones were respectively, Erastus, Andy, Arvilla, and William.

The next spring, having selected his farm, he removed thither with his family, and then commenced a life of toil and hardship such as falls to the lot of nearly every settler in a new country.

We will not attempt to follow them through these seventeen years, but come immediately to the year 1855, in which our story opens.

The little shingle shanty first erected has given place to the commodious log house, and that in turn to the tasteful frame building which now meets your gaze.

The slender, sickly husband has grown healthy and strong, the young wife has become the stately matron, and the children whom we first saw, young men and maidens. Other children have been added to the household, and they are now a family of ten, besides one pure bud which had been laid in an early grave. Prosperity has visited them, and their sons and daughters have grown up a blessing

Erastus, the eldest, is a bright, impulsive young man, who fills the house with life and fun. Andy is more quiet and sedate, thinking more of doing a kind action than of making sport. Arvilla, the eldest daughter, is married, and lives near her parents. William is a tall, handsome boy of nineteen. And now we come to Abigail, a girl of seventeen, and the heroine of our story. We cannot call her handsome, yet there is something in her bright black eyes and full red lips that makes her interesting. No one in those days would have selected her for a heroine. As it is not her beauty, but her disposition, that interests us, we will say no more about it.

It becomes necessary here to speak of her early childhood. At the age of ten years she made a public profession of religion. She had for years been a praying child, not the senseless form most children pray, but with a firm belief in the efficacy of prayer. Her mother, a truly pious woman, early strove to impress upon her mind the uselessness of prayer unless she believed in the power of God to hear and answer her prayer.

Many a pleasant hour have they spent while conversing upon this all-important subject, the mother striving to give her daughter a true understanding of the relations we bear toward our Creator, and the daughter treasuring up her every word, to be remembered in after years of darkness and trial. At one time, after a conversation of this nature, she received permission, with her little brother and sister, to go to Muddy Branch and slide on the ice. This was a great treat and the children were delighted. Owing to the stream being fed by living springs, it was much of the time unsafe, but as the cold had been intense for some days, it was considered safe. After being warmly wrapped up, they started off with happy hearts. On arriving at the crossing, what was their dismay to find that the ice, instead of presenting the smooth surface they had expected, was somewhat sunken in the middle and large cracks ran along the edge.

Abbie, not being enough of a philosopher to account for this by natural laws, was afraid to venture, and stood a long time thinking what to do. It was a severe disappointment to give up her sport. Her mother, she thought, would not have given her consent if it had not been safe, and yet she dared not trust herself upon the ice. At last, remembering the conversation of the morning, she fell upon her knees, and, telling God her fears, asked him to protect her and her brother and sister from harm. She rose from her knees with perfect faith that he had heard and would answer her prayer. Running upon the ice, she soon found, to her great joy, that it was firm. They were soon as happy as though no fear had entered their hearts.

That evening Abbie repeated the occurrence of the afternoon. Her wise mother, seeing that she was in danger of making a wrong use of her faith in God, tried to explain to her where she was at fault. She explained to her the cause of the cracks in the ice, told her it was really safe, and that the answer God had given her was not in making the ice more safe, but in taking the foolish fear from her heart.

"But," she continued, "if, on arriving at the spot, you had found the ice really unsafe, and had thrown yourself upon it, he would not have worked a miracle to save you. Besides, you would have displeased him by not making use of the reason he has given you. Remember, my dear child, that your reason was given you for a guide, and it is your duty to use it. You have no right to ask God to work a miracle to save you from the consequences of a rash act."

Abbie pondered upon her mother's words, and many times in after years she had cause to remember them. She did not lose her faith in prayer, but she strove to use the reason of which her mother had spoken. It is no wonder that, with such a wise teacher and her own desire to learn, coupled with the Spirit of God in her heart, she grew up a firm, consistent Christian.

We will spend no more time over the incidents of her childhood, but come immediately to our story.

CHAPTER II.

INCIDENTS OF GIRLHOOD DAYS.

MR. SAUNDERS' business had increased to such an extent that he was now obliged to hire much of his work done. Some favored hand was often taken into the house and treated as one of the family. About this time a young man by the name of Rushford came into the place looking for a home and work. He was the son of an old and valued friend of Mrs. Saunders, and was, accordingly, immediately hired by Mr. Saunders. Being a quiet, steady young man and faithful workman, he soon gained the respect of his employer and the good-will of his associates. As he was always treated as one of the family, he was often in the company of Abbie, who, knowing the mind of her father concerning the young man, treated him accordingly, and they were soon intimate friends. About this time a circumstance happened which, though amusing, caused a feeling of reserve, amounting to coldness, between them.

A small tenant house stood a short distance from the farmhouse. In this lived a Mr. Ferris with his wife and two little girls, and Mr. Elton and wife, uncle and aunt of Rushford's.

(16)

One day a poster was stuck up on the highway near Mr. Saunders' announcing a grand caravan and circus at W., a small railroad town about ten miles away. As it was the dull season of the year, several of the "hands" started in good season for the village. Among them went Mr. Elton, taking with him his young and handsome wife, and leaving behind a sister of Mrs. Elton's, Susie Jones, a girl of eighteen or nineteen.

Mrs. Ferris, who was somewhat of an invalid, had been more unwell than usual for a few days, and her sister, a pretty girl of nineteen, had come to nurse her.

Abbie, standing at the window of her room, saw Mr. Elton drive past, and, knowing where he was going, began to feel lonely as she thought of the gay time in store for them. Her brothers had gone away, after dressing with scrupulous care, evading her questions as to where they were going, and she had a vague idea they were then escorting their sweethearts to the show. Her father, who did not believe in shows, had gone to the village on business. (Strange how business happened to call him on that particular day!) In short, she was lonesome, and, thinking of Susie, who she knew was left alone, she started across the orchard to pay her a visit. She found her sitting by the window looking lonely enough.

"Good-morning, Susie," she said, as she entered the room; "you look as lonely as I feel this morn-

2

ing. I would like to shake that brother-in-law of
yours; I think it was too bad for him not to take
you."

"So do I," said Rachel Dorn, entering the room
at that moment; "if I had her sister here, I would
shake her."

"Oh, I don't care," said Susie, "only it is lonesome staying alone! Can't you come and stay with
me, Abbie, until they come back? We could have
such a nice visit."

"I should like to very much," answered Abbie,
"if mother can spare me."

"Of course she'll be glad to get rid of you," said
Susie, laughing; "you know you haven't done much
since you were sick."

"Indeed, I have been quite smart for a day or
two," replied Abbie; "I helped mother to-day until
everything was tidy, and then, as I stood by the
window watching the teams pass for the circus, she
said I had better run over and see you. I suppose
my face looked pretty long, I wanted so much to
go to the circus. They say there is a large menagerie with it, and I would so like to see the animals.
I have never seen one."

"Never been to a menagerie?" cried Rachel in
astonishment.

"No," said Abbie; "I remember when I was a
very little girl my uncle and aunt took me to a circus, but there was no menagerie with it."

Mrs. Ferris had heard what the girls said, and,

being a kind-hearted woman, sympathized with them in their disappointment. She knew her husband had stayed at home because she was not well enough to go with him. She at once made up her mind that he should go that evening and take the three girls. Calling them into the bedroom, she disclosed her plan.

The girls looked at each other in astonishment for a moment, and then Rachel said, "But, sister, will not the men think us bold to propose such a plan?"

"I will ask Henry myself," she answered; "surely I may be allowed that privilege without being called bold."

"But," continued Rachel, "Mr. Rushford is at work with him to-day, and I fear he will think we meant to give him a hint."

"I will manage that," said Mrs. Ferris.

And so it was agreed that they were to go if it could be arranged, and Abbie went home to consult her mother. Mrs. Saunders, not liking the plan, would not give her consent, and Abbie gave up going. She felt somewhat disappointed, but went immediately to tell the girls of her decision.

She found the family at dinner. Mr. Ferris said he would go if they would accept young Rushford as one of the party. To this they of course agreed, and all joined in regrets that Abbie could not be one of the party, Rushford saying he would not go if she did not. Abbie was sorry she had had anything to do with it. She seemed to be spoiling the pleasure of the whole party. The men soon returned to their work, while Abbie stayed a short time to chat with the other girls. They seemed very much disappointed, and said they would not enjoy their ride if she did not go.

She at last left them, feeling more sorry on their account than her own. She tried, by joining her mother in the afternoon work, to forget the occurrence of the morning. When all was finished, she went into her own room, took up her sewing, and sat down at the window. From where she sat she could see the spring from which the water for both houses was brought, the orchard, with its long, straight rows of choice fruit trees, and the tenant house, peeping out from among the leaves. She had not sat there long before she saw Mr. Rushford, apparently coming to the spring for water. He filled his canteen, and then, seeing Abbie at the window, he came up and said:—

"So you will not join our party to-night?"

"No," she answered, looking up, "though I am sorry to disappoint the girls."

"It will disappoint them," he said, "for Mr. Ferris says he will not go if I do not, and you know what I said at noon."

He waited a moment, but, receiving no answer, continued, "If you go, you will confer a great favor upon us all."

Abbie felt quite perplexed, but, after conferring

with her mother, decided to go.   As it was late, it
would be necessary to start in an hour.   Abbie
noticed that, as Mr. Rushford passed up the road,
he made a sign to Mr. Ferris, who soon left the field
and went to the house.

Abbie wasted no time, and was soon ready for
her ride.   While waiting for the carriage, and expecting every moment to see her young friends
appear at the door ready for their ride, she was
surprised to see Susie enter, in her home dress.   As
she caught sight of Abbie, she said, "So you are
going after all, are you?"

"Yes," she answered, " Mr. Rushford came and
persuaded me that it was my duty to go, as you were
all so anxious.   But you are not ready, Susie?   I
am expecting the carriage every moment, and was
afraid you would get started first."

"Oh, I shall be ready in time!" and with a look
that puzzled Abbie, she turned and left the room.

Abbie had not long to think of the strange, displeased look upon Susie's face.   The carriage soon
came, and they were speedily upon the road.

As they passed out of sight, Abbie wondered why
her friends did not start.   Her companion made an
evasive answer, and, seeing that she appeared ill at
ease, exerted himself to make her forget them, and
enjoy her ride.

They soon arrived at their destination, and, in
the bustle and confusion, Abbie gave up all hopes of
meeting them that evening, and gave herself up to

the enjoyment of the scene. To her the scene was
grand and beautiful. The great tent, with its brilliant lights, and rows of seats rising one above
another, filled with well-dressed men and women,
the cages of wild beasts, few of which she had ever
seen before, the kind attentions of her companion,
all combined to make her forget, for a time, at least,
the conviction that had been forcing itself upon her
mind that all was not right.

On the way home Mr. Rushford said he did not
think they had left home, and Abbie wondered
much what could have kept them. As she entered
her room, a short time after, her little sister awoke,
and seeing Abbie, said:—

"So you are back again, are you? Have you
had a pleasant time?"'

"Very pleasant," she answered, smiling.

"Well, I don't think you will have as pleasant a
time in the morning. They are all mad at you, up
at the other house. I went up there after you went
away, and found the girls crying, and Mrs. Ferris
declaring she would not have believed it of you
—deceitful thing—to pretend you did not want to go,
and then start off and cheat the girls out of their
ride. I asked why they did not go too. She said
Mr. Rushford had contrived it all, just because you
felt too proud to go with Rachel. Mr. Ferris tried
to take your part, but she would not listen to him,
saying she knew she was right, and Rachel should
never speak to you again. Then Rachel cried
harder than ever."

"But why did they not go?" asked Abbie. "I can't see how I hindered them."

"I don't know," said Mattie, sleepily. "You can ask them in the morning."

Abbie lay awake a long time, trying to think how she had interfered with them. At last she gave it up in despair, and was soon fast asleep.

She lost no time the next morning before calling upon her young friends, to ascertain, if possible, in what way she had offended them. She found Mrs. Ferris scolding, and she would not even answer Abbie's salutation, but strove, by a great show of dignity, to punish her for her slight. Abbie, who did not understand the cause of her wrath, was pained to see this, and turned toward the girls, who were both present, for an explanation. They both spoke to her. Susie looked hurt and defiant. Rachel's eyes were red with weeping, and as Abbie spoke, her tears flowed afresh. Poor Abbie stood as if stunned for a moment.

At length, gaining the command of her voice, she begged Rachel to tell her what she had done to deserve such treatment.

"What have you done?" interrupted Mrs. Ferris, indignantly. "I should think you would be ashamed to ask that question, after doing such a mean thing, and cheating the girls out of their ride."

Mr. Ferris gave her a warning look, but it only served to make her more indignant. "You may cringe down and bear it, if you want to," she cried

angrily, "I shall not, without giving her a piece of
my mind.   It was all a 'put-up job,' just because
Abbie feels too proud to go with the girls.   Rachel
is just as good as she is, if she is poor, instead of
being old Saunders' daughter."

There is no telling how much she might have
said had not Rachel, who was deeply grieved at the
turn affairs had taken, and pained at what her
sister said, risen, and, taking down her pail, started
to milk the cows, which stood in their yard, waiting
for her.

Abbie watched her until she disappeared, and
she felt that in her heart there was more grief than
anger.   Then, turning to Susie, she begged her to
tell her what was the matter.   In all that had been
said she could not tell where she had offended
them.   Susie, then, in as few words as possible,
told her that Mr. Ferris had engaged the only
team in the barn.   After Abbie had consented to
go, Mr. Rushford had gone to the old gentleman,
and, telling him that Mr. Ferris had given up going,
got permission to take the single horse and carriage, thereby spoiling Mr. Ferris' team.   Of course
there was nothing for them to do but give up going.

"Yes," said Mrs. Ferris, "and you needn't pretend ignorance.   It won't do any good.   I know it
was agreed to between you and Steve Rushford,
because you did not want to go with Rachel; but
you needn't be so smart; she is just as good as
you are."

Abbie was too surprised to answer. She saw at once what a strong web of circumstantial evidence was woven against her. Seeing there was no use of talking to Mrs. Ferris while in her present state of mind, she arose slowly and left the house. As she passed Mr. Ferris, their eyes met. His fell to the floor, while a blush overspread his face. She wondered at this for a moment, but other thoughts soon chased it from her mind. She felt sad that they should suspect her of complicity in such an act, but it grieved her most that Rachel should think she meant to slight her, whom she loved dearly, and she hastened to avow her innocence.

As she approached her, Rachel looked up quickly and then let her eyes fall again. She did not speak, but Abbie saw that her bosom heaved, and her tears fell fast. She could restrain herself no longer. Bursting into tears, she exclaimed: "O Rachel, do you then believe what your sister says? You cannot think I would be so mean!"

She could say no more, but wept in silence. Hers was no vain show of grief. At the first words Mrs. Ferris had spoken she had comprehended the cause of Rachel's grief, and full well did she know that if Rachel for a moment believed her sister's version of the affair, no words could express the grief she must feel, for, although among themselves she was called 'one of the girls,' young as she was, her lot had been one of deep trouble. About two years before this she had married the son of a wealthy farmer in the neighborhood, and for a time was happy. From this state she was rudely awakened by the disappearance of her young and fickle husband, leaving no clue to his destination. He left his young wife, who was shortly to become a mother, with only a small yearly allowance, to a lonely, anxious life. She was a sweet, gentle creature, beloved by all who knew her, and with many staunch friends, among the dearest of whom she had counted Abbie. Their tastes were much alike, and from their first acquaintance they had loved one another.

Abbie had heard her sad story, and had both felt and professed great sympathy for her. So far from feeling ashamed of her company, she was proud to be considered her friend, and would not, willingly, have given her a moment's pain. To be suspected of so open a slight was more than she could bear, and she determined, if possible, to remove the suspicion. Before she could speak, Rachel rose, and, clasping the hand of her young friend, said: "No, no, dear Abbie, do not grieve so. There is something wrong in all this, but in my heart I feel you are not to blame."

"Thank you, my dear friend," cried Abbie. "You have taken the heaviest part of the load from me. I am sorry the rest are angry with me, but I can bear that if you do not think me untrue to you."

"I now feel perfectly sure you have been true

to me, dear friend, but someone is in the wrong. And, O Abbie! you never can know what I have suffered since you drove away last night. It seemed to bring all my old trouble fresh to my mind, and the fear that you would prove untrue, as sister tried to make me believe, was almost more than I could bear. Yet I did not believe it, even then. When I saw you this morning, all doubt of you vanished."

"Thank you for your faith in me, dear Rachel," said Abbie; "but can you form no idea why Rushford should act as he did? He certainly gave me no hint that you were not going. I saw Mr. Ferris come back to the field from the house, and they seemed to be talking earnestly for a few minutes. Then Rushford took the pail, and, coming to the spring, set it down, came to the window where I sat, and asked, as a favor, that I would change my mind and go. I supposed that you had decided not to go unless I did, so, after consulting mother, I told him I would go. He turned hurriedly away, saying he would be there with the carriage in an hour, and I rose to prepare for my ride, supposing I had removed the only barrier to your enjoyment. When Susie came in, I was very much surprised at her manner and at her not being dressed for the ride. But she made no explanation, and, the carriage coming just then, I had no time to find out what it meant. I wondered at his taking a single carriage instead of going with you, but, not liking to ask, I said nothing and we drove away. I asked if you would start soon, and he answered that you were not ready yet. I felt disappointed, but said no more, although I kept watch for you. He must have known that I was looking for you, but he made no explanation. So now you know what happened as well as I can tell you. It looks to me as if I was not only deceived, but that it was intentional. The object I cannot even guess."

"It is strange," said Rachel. "I cannot understand it. Will you come in?" she said as they approached the house.

"No," said Abbie, "I must go now. Cannot you come over soon? I want you to help me unravel the mystery."

"I will. Good-morning."

As Rachel entered the room, she was surprised to see her sister in tears, and hear her brother-in-law say: "Well, you hadn't orter have talked to her that way, nohow. You'll lose me my place with that tongue of yours, if you ain't careful. And then what'll we do? I don't know another man that'd give me the chance Saunders has. By the great guns! why can't a woman hold her tongue? The gals would 'a been mad, but they'd 'a forgot it in a few days, if you hadn't 'a said nothing."

"I thought she meant to insult Rachel," said Mrs. Ferris, sobbing, "and I wasn't going to stand it."

"Oh, by the great guns!" ejaculated Mr. Ferris, rising, and leaving the room hastily, for he hated a scene.   In fact, it was the fear of such an emergency that had caused him to do as he had.

Susie no longer looked angry, but decidedly amused.   As she left the room, Rachel followed her, anxious to know what it all meant.   On entering her own room, Susie threw herself into a chair, and burst into an uncontrollable fit of laughter.

"What in the world is the matter?" asked Rachel. "I cannot see why you should laugh at such a time as this."

"At such a time as this," gasped Susie, laughing more than ever.   "Do you know what a noble brother-in-law you have, and what a precious set of fools we have been?"

"I cannot understand what you mean," said Rachel, rather inclined to be angry.   She could not see what there was to be laughed at.

"So you don't," said Susie.   "I suppose I must tell you."

She then told her all Mr. Ferris had said after Abbie left the room.   As she listened, a look of relief came over Rachel's face, followed by one of satisfaction, as she saw that no slight had been intended to her, or anyone else, and that Abbie was entirely cleared from suspicion.

"I must go and tell her," she said.

Returning to her sister's room, she put things to rights, and, leaving her sister comfortable, hastened

to her young friend. She found her looking troubled
and sad. She looked up as Rachel entered, and,
seeing her smiling face, exclaimed:—

"O Rachel, you have good news to tell, I am
sure!"

"Yes, you dear, tender-hearted little girl, I have.
And now please drive away that troubled look,
which you need no longer wear, and listen to me,
for I have quite an amusing story to tell," she continued, seating herself near by. "It seems that my
precious brother-in-law did not relish the idea of
being toted off by a couple of giddy girls to the
caravan, perhaps fearing he must foot the bill for
the crowd. So, after they returned to the field, he
asked Rushford if he was in earnest in saying what
he did at the dinner table.

"'To what do you refer?' asked Rushford.

"'That you would not go if Miss Saunders did not.'

"'I certainly am. That would be my only attrac-
tion, and as she will not go, I shall not.'

"'Oh, come, now!' entreated Ferris; 'say you
will go. Either of the other girls would be proud
of you as an escort. Besides, how's a fellow to take
care of two girls in a crowd like that, I'd like to
know?'

"But Rushford refused to have anything to do
with it. After a few minutes' silence, Ferris said:—

"'I say, Steve, I have it. I suppose if that little
black-eyed midget will go, you don't care a fig for
the rest?'

"'No; what then'?

"'Well, you can just go and get the horse and carriage and take her. Father has but one team in the stable to-day, so if you get the single carriage of course I can't take the double one. So you see that will serve me and yourself too.'

"'But do you suppose she would go?'

"'In course she'd go,' said Ferris. 'I know these gals better'n you do, and I know she'd go.'

"'But if your plan works, the other girls will be down on us. I don't think she will go on that account.'

"'Don't tell her, then. She'll find it out soon enough. I guess you've a right to take her, if you want to.'

"Seeing that Steve still hesitated, he continued: 'I'll go down to the house and see how things look, and if I think it'll do, I'll tell you.'

"He crossed the field and entered the house unseen. He heard Susie say:—

"'I am so sorry Abbie is not going,' and me say, 'So am I. I should not have thought of going but for her. I would rather she had the pleasure than to have it myself.'

"Ferris slipped quietly away, and, returning to the field, related what he had heard, and told Rushford to go ahead.

"'If I only thought,' he said, musingly.

"'Don't stop to think,' interrupted Ferris. 'You can't more than get the mitten, and that won't hurt you any.'

"The young man turned hastily, took up the pail, and the rest you already know. There," she added, rising, and kissing the young girl affectionately, " I have made quite a story of it. Now you must promise to forgive my kind-hearted but blundering brother-in-law, and my sister for speaking so to you, and we shall all be friends again."

Abbie gave the desired promise and Rachel returned home. But Abbie was still troubled. She did not like the course Rushford had taken. She could but acknowledge that if he had told her how things stood, she would have refused to go at once. But then she would have respected him, while now she felt she must distrust him. Had he told her when she inquired, after starting, that they were not coming, she could not have blamed him so much, for, as she did not ask about them when he invited her, he was under no obligations to explain. Instead of doing this, he had intentionally deceived her, and had, by so doing, given pain to her dear friend, and caused her to be thought ill of. "But," she thought, "he did it entirely for my pleasure; I must therefore forgive his blunder." She herself had been in the wrong in allowing her foolish thoughts to be known. She resolved to be more prudent in the future, and to think no more of the unpleasant occurrence. She did not for a moment think that he could desire to be her lover; the thought would have frightened her. No, it was only as a friend, and because he thought it would give her pleasure. In spite of this, it left an impression upon her mind that she could not trust him implicitly.

Though she did not think she had changed her manner towards him, he felt a coldness which not only chilled but piqued him, and he vowed he would make her repent, if it took a lifetime. While cherishing these thoughts, he redoubled his exertions to please her parents, and gain her affections, for he loved the young and unsuspecting girl as well as his selfish nature would permit. From that day he swore to make her his wife, by fair means or by foul. He meant no real evil in this threat, but such was his disposition that, if thwarted in a pet scheme, he must have revenge, even though the person offending him be his best friend.

He knew that he had willfully deceived her, but as it had harmed no one, he did not see why she should be offended, forgetting that evil should never be done that good may come of it, for this had never been one of his mottoes.

Abbie, unconscious of his thoughts, and never imagining the ride as anything but an act of friendly courtesy, intended to give her pleasure, and no more than he would have done for any other girl under the same circumstances, remembered how freely she had given expression to her disappointment, and felt, she could not have told why, a sense of embarrassment in his presence. In her utter lack of knowledge of the ways of the world, she did not attempt to conceal her embarrassment, but avoided him whenever she could without being rude.

He saw that she strove to avoid him, and his pride was stung, though he had no thought of changing his intentions toward her. So it happened that the circumstance which would otherwise have served to make them more social, only drove them farther apart.

Rushford was obliged to see the position he longed to hold filled by an old friend of her childhood, whom Abbie had long known and loved, though, he being but two years her senior, they had never assumed the position of lovers.

Charley Reynolds was a very good type of the country boy. He was strong and robust, with laughing eyes, sunny hair, and a heart full of love for all God's creatures. Abbie could hardly remember the first pleasant stroll they had taken together, when he used to help her over all the rough places, and climb the bluffs after the flowers she loved.

They had grown up together, he according to her the many courtesies which a loving heart prompts, and she accepting them with childish confidence. Little suspecting that jealous eyes were watching them, they took no pains to conceal their regard. Rushford saw that if he gained the hand of the girl, he must supplant young Charley.

CHAPTER III.

CHARLEY REYNOLDS.

THUS matters stood for two years. Stephen Rushford still lived with Mr. Saunders through the busy season, and at an uncle's in the neighborhood during the rest of the time. He was waiting for a favorable opportunity to press his suit. She, all unconscious of his intentions, was growing more and more conscious that she loved Charley Reynolds, and that he was the handsomest young man in Greenvale.

His father, a kind old gentleman, had sometimes jokingly called her his daughter, and intimated rather plainly what he hoped would happen some day, if Charley knew what he was about. She became suspicious, by some remarks her father had made, that he too considered the match made and was pleased with it.

As for Charley, he had long looked upon Abbie as belonging to himself exclusively, and did not dream that anyone would dispute his claims, or that she could refuse him when he should ask her to become his bride.

Thus these two years had passed away, when Charley Reynolds and William Saunders decided to

go West with Erastus and Anda to take up claims.
Charley thought when he should become a landed
proprietor he need hesitate no longer to claim his
bride.   He did not dream of failure ; bright pictures
of his future in the far West, in a home of his own,
made beautiful by his own hand, flitted through his
brain.   Then, with Abbie as his wife, what more
could he ask ?

At the earnest request of her eldest brother,
Abbie, with a younger sister, obtained permission to
accompany the young fortune hunters to their new
homes and visit some old friends in the vicinity.

Charley heard of this arrangement with delight.
He should not have to leave his sweetheart, even for
a short time.   As he would be able to see her often,
he determined to know his fate as soon as his home
should be selected.

The journey was a pleasant one, and all went
merry as a marriage bell.   The young men selected
their claims, stuck their stakes, and began the work
necessary to secure them.   Young Reynolds felt
that all he desired to make him happy was to hear
the words from Abbie's lips that would give him
the right to claim her as his own.

Until now he had not feared what the result would
be, but, as the time approached, he felt a strange
misgiving at his heart, a sudden trembling for which
he could not account.   Could it be that he had deceived himself, that she did not love him, as he had
hoped.   He thought of the past.   She had always

seemed to prefer his society, and had never seemed
to care for another. He felt sure Stephen Rushford
loved her, but she had never seemed to care for him.
Feeling that he was wronging her by his doubts, he
resolved to conquer them and know his fate ere
another day should dawn. Little did he dream of
the disappointment that awaited him, nor of the
poison that was even then working against him.

Had he spoken a day sooner, the answer would
have been favorable. But within the last few days
Abbie had heard reports that had made her angry
with him, and when he called she met him so
coldly that he almost lost courage. At last he
spoke, and received a decided refusal. This in turn
angered him, and, believing her a heartless flirt, he
left her. The subject was never renewed, and thus
two more hearts that had been faithful for years
were parted by a silly lovers' quarrel.

Abbie soon repented of her foolish anger, but had
not courage to confess her fault. He would not
renew his suit, though he had loved her long and
well, and thus, drifting farther and farther apart,
they returned to their homes in Illinois, when Abbie
took up her duties again with a sad heart.

On the first evening of her return she met Mr.
Rushford at the supper table. He gave her a
quick, searching glance, at which she was rather
annoyed, and then became uncommonly cheerful,
saying it seemed like home once more. He asked
a great many questions about the West, and said
he thought of going soon to see for himself.

"Plenty of land, I suppose?" he asked, turning to Erastus.

"Oh, yes," was the reply, "plenty of land now, but settling up fast!"

"Any more joining you?" asked his father.

"Yes, one-quarter section. Splendid land! I could hardly choose between that and mine."

"I have been thinking," continued Mr. Saunders, "that if you are all going I might as well sell out and go along. I would have money, and with your young hands to work, perhaps we could make it work 'round all right in the end."

"That would be splendid!" they all cried in a breath.

"Yes," he added, "I have been thinking of it a good deal since you went away. We can drive all our stock with us. I hate to have you all go and leave me. What do you think of it, my girl?" turning to Abbie. "Don't you like the West?"

"Very well, thank you," she answered, her face crimsoning, as she saw all eyes turned upon her, for she knew of what they were thinking.

"I thought so," he said mischievously. "I suppose you'll be asking me to let you go whether I do or not."

Abbie would have given anything to have stopped this speech. She glanced timidly at Steve (for so they now called him). She would not have cared so much if he had not been there. But he was occupied with his supper and did not look up.

She tried to form words to answer him carelessly, but she could not speak, and, rising, left the table and the room.

"Whew!" said her father, surprised at her manner, at the same time looking at Erastus. "What does it mean? She didn't seem to relish the joke."

Raz gave him a warning look, and he subsided into silence. Steve soon rose and left the room. Then Raz told his father that there was something wrong between Abbie and Charley, and as it pained her to speak of it, they had better not say anything about it.

"Just as you think," said Mr. Saunders, "but I hope it is nothing but a lovers' •quarrel that will soon blow over. Charley is a splendid fellow, and I counted on his going West with us."

None of them paid any attention to Steve, who did not return to the house until after the chores were done. He was very quiet and soon went to his room. The next day Mr. Saunders went away and returned at night with the intelligence that he had found a purchaser for Olney farm, and they might commence active preparations for the journey.

It was now the beginning of August, and as they wished to start by the middle of October, there was no time to be lost. There was, indeed, plenty of work to be done. The grain, which now dotted the fields in yellow shocks, must be gathered in, threshed, and taken to market. The other produce had never seemed so abundant as now, when it must all be disposed of in so short a time.

Indoors the same hurry and bustle prevailed. Mr. Saunders, who, the neighbors said, could keep an army at work, completely outdid himself, and there was no end to the good things to be prepared for them to eat. Never did men eat so before, and breakfast, dinner, and supper followed one another in quick succession.

If it had not been for Abbie's ready fingers, what would have become of the little Saunderses, who must all be provided with new clothing?

Roxy, who was four years younger than Abbie, was wide-awake with anticipation, and flew from one thing to another with startling rapidity, now assisting the kitchen maid to wash that great pile of dishes, but dropping the towel before it was half done, to see if Abbie was going to put a ruffle on her dress. She liked them so much. To her this was a small request, but to Abbie's more experienced mind it suggested many additional stitches. So she looked at her mischievously, saying she might if Roxy would hem them. But Roxy said hurriedly:—

"Oh, no, I haven't time; besides, I hate hemming!" and ran away to see how the men were getting along in the field.

Abbie smiled and said: "I thought that would settle it. Roxy hates sewing."

"No more than I did when I was a girl," said

her mother. "I would rather do any amount of housework than make my own clothes."

"I don't see how you could feel so. I would rather sew than do anything else."

"It is well you like it. There is surely enough to do."

"Yes," said Abbie, thoughtfully, "there is certainly enough to do. Roxy must have dress, cloak, and hat. Then there is Joe, Eddie, and Gussie must have full suits, to say nothing of the baby or ourselves. But don't worry, mother," she added cheerfully, "my task is not half as difficult as yours."

Her mother watched the busy fingers with wonder and admiration. She had always tried to perform her several duties, but sewing had been distasteful to her. As her eldest daughter had been like herself, she was pleased to see this daughter take to the disagreeable work with so much pleasure. She had long ago begun to trust the family sewing to her. She rose with a sigh of relief, and left the room to attend to some household duties, and Abbie was left alone.

Her fingers were busy, and so were her thoughts with the ever-recurring subject of her quarrel with Charley. She had long since come to the conclusion that there was some mistake in the reports, and that, but for her silly anger, the tangled web might have been straightened. Never before had his love seemed so dear to her as now, when it was beyond her reach.

She thought of the many happy hours they had spent together, and felt that he was justly angry with her. She ought not to have refused him in that haughty manner without giving some reason for her conduct; but she had done so, and it was now too late. She could not break over the false barrier custom had raised forbidding woman to plead her own cause in such matters.

Had she been able to lift the veil of the future, she might yet have saved herself ere it was indeed too late. She well knew that one sentence from her lips would bring him again to her side, but the false impression she had thus early imbibed sealed her lips, and that sentence was never spoken. Even then the shadow of coming sorrow settled upon her soul. They were weary, weary days that she passed at her work.

CHAPTER IV.

THE FAMILY MOVE WEST.

Y degrees the pile of work decreased, the grain was all disposed of, the cattle were all collected within the ten-acre lot, three huge wagons were drawn up near the house and covered with canvas, and their household goods were stowed away. Many valued articles of furniture must be left behind on account of room. One in particular, a table made and presented to Mrs. Saunders by her brother, who had moved to California, caused a great deal of disappointment. In vain did she plan and plead; it would not go in.

Indeed it is doubtful if all the little Saunderses could have been crowded into the space left for them; this, however, was not necessary. Joe declared he was not going to be stowed away with the women—not he. He was going to help drive the cattle, like Steve and Raz, so they needn't worry about him. And Roxy had begged the privilege of riding Fan, her favorite, and helping drive the cows. She had seen a girl do it when some emigrants went by, and she thought it was fun.

They were at last ready to start; the good-byes had all been spoken. As they passed out into the

road, the boys gave one loud whoop, then three
cheers for Minnesota, and they were on the road.
As they passed out of the lane to the prairie, Roxy
and Joe rendered such efficient aid in driving the
cattle that no one was sorry they had had their
own way. They received so much praise that they
were highly elated, and did not stop to think that
they were looking their last on dear, familiar scenes.
Not so Mrs. Saunders and Abbie. They realized
but too well the sadness of the parting. It was not
until the shades of evening warned them that camp-
ing-time was near that their faces lost their sad
looks. Then there was enough to do besides re-
pine. The little ones were tired and sleepy, and
wanted to go home. They were very much surprised when told that "camping out" meant to
sleep on the ground in a tent.

"What is a tent?" said little Gussie.

"It is a house made of cloth," said Abbie. " Papa
and the boys will put it up soon. If you won't cry,
you can see them."

Gussie wiped his eyes and tried to look brave.
As the work of putting up the tent soon commenced,
the homesick feeling was forgotten in the nov-
elty and excitement of the scene. All were tired
and hungry, and when Eddie remarked, at the table
of boards, that the supper was "real good," no one
felt like disputing his word. This was not the only
hearty meal eaten on that trip. The days were
spent in traveling and admiring the scenery. At

night they would stop in some wild, romantic spot, and the tired animals were allowed to graze, or lie down to rest, while the children sprang from the wagon, glad to use their little feet once more. The camp fire was built, the supper got, the tents pitched, and the beds prepared. There seemed no time to think of home. To judge from the happy faces, there was no inclination, yet Abbie often thought how happy she might have been if it had not been for her foolish pride and anger.

When the quiet Sabbath had come, everything seemed to be at rest, for Mr. Saunders would not travel on that day. The cattle were still allowed their liberty, and the tents were not moved. In front of one sat the father and mother, while near them the little ones were gathered, amusing themselves in one of the thousand ways of little children.

Abbie had grown tired of reading, and when Mr. Rushford proposed a stroll, she was glad to go. Their path led up a quiet stream for a short distance, and then, climbing a steep declivity, they stood on the point of a high bluff.

Beneath them lay the camp, in quiet serenity; beyond it the long bridge over which they had crossed; still farther on rose the hills, studded with trees, and over all the sun sinking in the far west. It was a splendid picture, well calculated to inspire the tenderest feelings of the heart. They unconsciously yielded to its influence, and, gazing far out over the beautiful landscape, thoughts of the far-off future filled their minds. Abbie wondered what good it had in store for her.

As they gazed, Rushford talked to her, in low, gentle tones, first of the scenery, and then of his childhood's home. He gave a glowing description of his home in Wisconsin. He spoke of his mother and sister, and wished Abbie could know them. And all this in such a quiet, easy way that Abbie was both surprised and pleased. She wondered that she could have thought him uninteresting, and when they returned to the camp, she no longer shunned him. He seemed so changed, so kind and thoughtful of the comfort of those around him. She wondered she had not noticed it before, and felt that she had been unjust to him.

The next day they started again on their journey, refreshed by their Sabbath's rest. Ere another rolled around, they were at home.

"Is this home?" said little six-year-old Eddie. "I don't see no house. Shall we live in the cloth house for ever'n ever?"

"Oh, no!" said Abbie, by whose side he sat. "There is a house in that clump of trees yonder. It is built of logs, and has only one room."

"Then where'll we sleep? Oh, there it is! I can see the top now. Oh, ain't it funny!" he added as they came nearer.

"It don't look a bit like our house," said Gussie.

The children all looked eager, and as they drew up to the door, Gussie exclaimed, "Why, mother, it's just logs of wood piled up like our cob houses!"

"THERE IS A HOUSE IN THAT CLUMP OF TREES YONDER."

"That's so," said Eddie, "only it ain't got any fence round it. We always make one."

"Yes, and we'll soon make one too," said Raz, smiling. "Can you tell us how?"

"Oh, yes! It is just as easy as can be, but I couldn't lift the logs," he added, dropping his look of importance.

"Oh, no," said his brother, laughing, "we will make some rails out of the logs! But now for supper in our new home. How do you like it?" turning to Roxy, who stood looking around with a dissatisfied air.

"I don't like it a bit, that's all! It isn't a bit nice, and I wish we were at home."

"So we are, little sister, and we will soon make it look like home, too. Come, let us work with a will."

He caught up an ax and went to work with such vigor that he soon had a bright fire in the stove which stood in one corner of the room.

As Abbie had said, the house had but one room, but it had the advantage of being very large. A homemade basswood table stood against the wall. The provisions were brought in, and while mother prepared supper, the beds were unpacked, and two bedsteads filled two respective corners, while the rest of the bedding was carried into the chamber, to be used by the boys.

By the time these arrangements were completed, supper was ready. They all ate with great relish.

The evening that followed was a busy and pleasant one. And so life commenced at their new home.

In the morning all was bustle and confusion. There was so much to be done. Another room must be built for a cook room; a barn must be built for the horses, and more hay cut for the cattle. As it was now the middle of October, there was no time to be lost.

Mr. Saunders could have commanded a larger army than ever now. He must, however, be content with the force then in command, which consisted of Raz and Will Saunders, Steven Rushford, Mr. Elton, who, with his young wife, had come with them, and was considered one of the family, and little Joe, who was eleven years old, and who had come to the conclusion that traveling, camping out, and driving cattle was hard work, and that he was "the worst bossed of all," as he had to run on errands for all hands.

All were soon at work. By the time the kitchen was built, the barn and sheds prepared, and the hay cut, the weather, which had been very mild, began to change. The nights were cold, with heavy frost. By the 20th of November, dark clouds overspread the sky, and all saw that an early snowstorm threatened them, while ten acres of turnips which had been sown on the new breaking, were still out. Two teams and four men were needed to haul in the hay. That left one team and two boys for turnips. The boys were both needed

to pull. Who would drive the team? It was here
Roxy's horsemanship came in play again. She immediately volunteered to drive the team, and was
gladly accepted. To work they went with a will.
By the time dinner was ready, a large pile of yellow turnips lay by the barn.

Abbie knew they must all be topped and put
under cover before the storm, or they would be
frozen. It did not look as if this could be accomplished, but she could try, and, gaining her mother's
consent, she called Annie and Joe and set to work.
The weather was disagreeable, with raw winds and
scarcely any sun. Though the storm held off for
several days, the work was not completed when,
one morning, Abbie found herself unable to rise.
The exposure had been too much for her health,
which was never good, and she was for many days
confined to her bed. She had the satisfaction, however, of knowing that, with the assistance she had
given, the turnips would be saved. She bore her
illness with great patience, and, with her mother's
tender nursing, was soon convalescent.

The storm had come. The men were gathered
around the cheerful fire. The boys, full of fun and
frolic, felt the confinement, and were rather noisy.
Abbie, still very weak, often, growing weary of the
noise, would go into the kitchen and sit by the
large stove, listlessly watching her mother as she
passed busily to and fro, and longing for the return
of strength that she might assist her. Steve would

4

frequently leave his companions, and, sitting by her side, strive to while away the tedium of the hours by reading to her or conversing, in low, gentle tones. By the time she had become strong and able to perform her usual duties, she had become very much attached to him.

Mrs. Saunders, who had known and loved his mother years before, was not displeased that they should become friends, and placed no obstacle in their path. When, a few weeks later, he asked her to be his wife, he met with few objections, for, after talking with Abbie, even Mr. Saunders forbore to check their happiness by his doubts.

True, he tried to persuade them to wait at least a year, but, finding them unwilling to listen, he at last gave his consent, and an early day was set for the wedding. He did not like the turn affairs had taken. He had never thought of Rushford as a son-in-law; besides, he was not pleased with the course he had taken since coming West. When he had proposed coming with them to this new country, he had talked of taking land. But, though there were several claims vacant in the neighborhood, he had taken no pains to secure one. He seemed content with the small wages Mr. Saunders could give him, without a seeming thought of doing more, or providing for the future.

Mr. Saunders was better acquainted with him than the rest of the family were. He knew him to have a cruel, relentless disposition, and he trembled

at the thought of placing his daughter's happiness
in his hands. Although he seemed honest and industrious, he had no settled principles, and Mr.
Saunders knew it, and feared for the consequences
of this step. He felt displeased with his daughter
for loving such a man, and displeased with himself
for consenting to the match. More than once he
nearly decided to break it up. Had he known the
true state of Abbie's mind, he would have done so,
but she had not confided in him, or anyone, and,
fearing he might make matters worse, he kept his
own counsel. When, a few days before the wedding, he received an important business call which
would detain him from home for two or more
weeks, he was almost glad to go.

The trip must be made with his team, and, the
day before starting, while at the breakfast table,
Abbie heard him express a wish for a pair of home-
knit wool gloves to drive in. Immediately after
breakfast her mother was surprised to see Abbie
winding yarn, instead of working at her trousseau.

"Why, what are you doing?" she asked in surprise.

"Father wants a pair of gloves," Abbie answered
quietly.

"But you cannot spare the time from your own
work now, my child. Besides, you cannot finish
them in time."

"Oh, yes, I can! Don't you remember, I made
me a pair of mittens in a day last winter?"

"But there is more work in a pair of gloves, and these must be larger," said her mother, looking anxiously at the large pile of sewing on the table, and thinking that Abbie's hands must do it all.

"Oh, do not object, dear mother! When father comes back, I shall be married, you know, and not free to do his bidding. He shall have his gloves if I work all night and wear my old cloak besides. But I shall finish them in time, you will see."

Her mother said no more, but returned to her work. Many a time she had denied herself some pleasure, and worked until the "wee small hours" to accomplish this same weary task, without a thought that she had done anything worthy of praise, but that Abbie should of her own free will do so now seemed to her a fresh token of her loving heart. But Abbie did not think of this. Her heart had been filled with compunction because she had not taken her father's advice, especially as he had not said a word against her lover, but had only asked for a delay.

She saw that she had been hasty and selfish, and feared he would doubt her love for him. She longed for some way to show him that she still loved him, and when he expressed this wish, she determined it should be gratified.

To be sure, she had enough to do. There was her dress, not finished (Abbie never thought of wearing one she had not made with her own hands), her cloak to be trimmed and stitched, besides the "hundred and one" other things to be done. But she put them resolutely away, and, taking her needles, sat down to her self-imposed task. All day long she plied her needles. When the short winter day was done, and the men were gathered for their evening meal, she had only commenced the thumb of the second glove.

Abbie's heart almost failed her. The task had been greater than she had anticipated. The yarn was fine, which made a greater number of stitches necessary. Her hands ached. Her fingers had been worn to the quick, and every stitch now taken gave her fresh pain. But she never paused, until, as the clock struck ten, the last stitch was taken.

Never while her life lasts will she forget that evening. The pain made her quiet and thoughtful. Each stitch caused a fresh pang of pain, yet how small a space it filled in the glove! She wondered if this piece of work was a shadow of her life. She had begun for pleasure; she had continued for duty; she had ended in pain. Would it be so with her life? The thought made her shudder. But why should such thoughts come to her at this time? No, she would not believe it. She had refused a request of her father's, and had done this to show that it was not for lack of love for him, and to punish herself for this first disobedience.

Alas, she knew not how small a portion of her punishment was found in this act! Many a bitter tear must be shed, many a pain must be endured, ere her punishment was complete.

Before she was awake in the morning, her father was gone, and she resumed her work with greater pleasure than she would have felt had he gone without his gloves.

CHAPTER V.

THE wedding day arrived at last, clear and beautiful. The last stitch had been taken. Abbie, robed in her bridal attire, stood by her mother's side, receiving her blessing and advice. But she was not happy, she knew not why. Since that night when the thought that she was weaving her own destiny came to her, she had had strange forebodings of evil. It seemed so lonely without her father. She had never felt so before in his absence, but now she seemed to need him to protect her from some unknown danger.

There seemed to her to have been a sudden change in her lover. He seemed less gentle and loving, and once, when he stood watching her, she looked up suddenly and saw, or fancied she saw, a strange look in his face—a something that struck a chill to her heart! It was only for a moment, then he had spoken some light words and walked away.

But that look had haunted her ever since. It brought back all her old distrust, long since forgotten. Just now all seemed to be dark ahead. She wondered if all girls felt as she did. Yes,

(55)

probably they did. She would not trouble her mother with her fears. She was only nervous.

They stood thus, silent and still, when the sleigh was announced. As her mother released her hand she said, "Trust in God, my child."

How these simple words startled her! She seemed to hear them for the first time. Had she trusted in God to guide her in the step she was about to take? Alas! now that it was too late she knew she had not. In a moment the last five months of her life seemed spread like a scroll before her. She seemed to have lived in a daze since her quarrel with Charley, and to have been led on by some cruel power the source of which she could not guess. She seemed to have forgotten even to pray. She had said her prayers, but had she really prayed? The thought made her tremble. She longed to stop and think, but it was too late. The gay crowd were leading her away, with smiling faces.

As they handed her into the sleigh, she met the eyes of her lover. They were filled with such a soft, tender light as he leaned over her to adjust the robes, that her fear all vanished like dew. As they skimmed lightly over the crisp snow, and while the horses' feet kept time to the merry jingle of the bells, a sweet peace and trust stole over her, and she was happier than she had been for many days.

The five miles' drive was soon accomplished, and

the bridal party was ushered into the cozy parlor of the pastor, whose family were all collected to witness the ceremony.

They took their places, while the pastor reverently knelt and offered up a fervent prayer for the blessing of God upon the pair who were about to be united in the holy bonds of wedlock. Then he arose and began slowly to repeat the words which were to bind them together.

Abbie scarcely seemed to breathe until, in answer to the words, "Do you solemnly swear to take this woman for your lawful wedded wife, to love, cherish, and protect her, as long as you both shall live?" Rushford pronounced the words, "I do." Something in the tone startled her, so that she scarcely heard the rest of the service. What could it mean? Why should she be so startled? What was there in his tone and manner that had seemed to thrill every nerve with terror, and strike a chill, as of death, to her heart?

She was so preoccupied as to forget where she was, until the pastor's playful salute to the bride roused her to a sense of her position. Her friends kindly greeted her, and many jokes went round.

After a pleasant half hour, they set out for home, where they arrived at dark, and found a plentiful meal awaiting them, to which they did ample justice.

Several friends had joined the family, and, amid their merry jokes, the time passed pleasantly. Late in the evening Abbie found herself alone with her husband, standing in the large kitchen. They could hear the merry voices and peals of laughter in the room where the guests, who were in high glee, were assembled. All at once there was a hush. The outer door opened, and the clear voice of Will was heard saying:—

"Good-evening, Mr. Weir, come in, come in. You are late."

What Mr. Weir said in answer, Abbie did not hear, for she had been again startled by the appearance of her husband. At the first sound of that name he had started and turned pale. A bright glitter came into his eyes, as he stood staring wildly toward the door that led to the room from which the sounds came. At the sound of Weir's voice, he sprang forward and locked the door, then turned a look of wild triumph at his frightened wife.

Hearing the voice again, he began pacing the floor excitedly, muttering between his set teeth, "What fiend sent him here, to-night of all nights?"

So wild and fierce was his look and manner that Abbie stood spellbound. Her blood seemed frozen in her veins, and she could neither move nor speak. She heard someone try the door. Then her brother called playfully to them not to eat too much, as it was a bad notion for children—going to the cupboard in the evening. Then a laugh followed.

Abbie heard all this, vaguely, as she watched the

excited movements of her husband. She seemed
to live an age in those few minutes. Suddenly her
mother's words came to her mind, "Trust in God,
my child." Her heart rose to God in prayer, and
a sweet peace came to her. Her whole being
seemed filled with tender love for her husband, and
she walked slowly toward him. He had paused in
his rapid walk, and, as she approached him, looked
at her in a bewildered way. She laid her hand
gently on his arm. At that moment Will shook the
door vigorously, saying, "Come, open the door, or
there'll be no pie for breakfast."

Steve started to obey, but, finding it locked, he
turned to his wife with a strange, bewildered look,
asking, "Why is it locked?"

"Oh, just for a joke! Open it," she answered, so
calmly that she wondered at herself.

He obeyed, and they entered the room amid the
laughter of the guests. Abbie watched her husband nervously, as Mr. Weir stepped gallantly forward, and grasped first her hand, and then that of
her husband. He took the proffered hand with no
visible signs of emotion, greatly to the surprise of
Abbie, who scarcely took her eyes from his face for
the rest of the evening. But nothing more happened to arouse her fears, though the impression,
which in that dreadful moment had come home to
her heart, that her husband was insane, did not
leave her. This impression was strengthened by
another strange occurrence which happened the
next day.

As she stood alone in the shade near the house, he had approached her, with that strange glitter in his eyes, and asked her to take a walk. Fearing to cross him, she complied, and he led her a wild chase through the grove, then across a clearing into the woods, through which he tramped, with no seeming object, keeping her close to his side, and seeming angry and excited when she failed to keep pace with him.

After performing a large circle, they neared the house. All at once he seemed conscious of his whereabouts, looked bewildered, and, turning to her, asked what had happened. She answered lightly that they had been taking a walk. He gazed into her eyes for a moment, while his filled with an exultant light, and then left her and rejoined the men, while she, with a beating heart, entered the house.

When he came in in the evening, he did not appear to remember their strange walk. He was as gentle and thoughtful as usual of her comfort, assisted her with the evening's work, and, to all appearances, was as sane as anyone. But this was not to last. Two days did not pass away before she was awakened about four o'clock in the morning, with the request to get up quick, and go with him.

"Where do you wish to go?" she asked, in surprise.

"Over there," he answered. "Come, make haste."

"Oh, no!" she said soothingly, for he trembled

violently and seemed greatly agitated. "It is dark, and very cold. We do not want to go until daylight."

"Yes, yes. Come now," pulling her by the arm. "Make haste, or it will be too late."

He was perfectly wild with excitement. She arose mechanically, to obey his request. She tried to speak, but her voice failed her. Her courage had all forsaken her, and she dared not disobey. She wondered what he could want. Where could he wish her to go at this time of night? What was he going to do with her? Perhaps lead her to some lonely spot, and—oh, horrors! what a thought! She could not, would not go. Yet, as she felt his eyes fixed upon her, she dared not disobey.

Suddenly, like an inspiration, came her mother's words, "Trust in God, my child." She closed her eyes, and raised her heart to God in prayer for guidance. It was indeed a trying moment. But God, who hears the ravens when they cry, did not forsake her now. All fear left her heart. Her mind became clear, and she saw how absurd was the request, and what a wild act her obedience would be. He still watched her with his baleful eyes, but she did not quail.

"Come," he said, taking her hand.

"No, I cannot go." Her tone was calm and firm. "I dare not go."

"You do not love me, then? You will not obey me?"

"Steven," she said firmly, "I will do anything in reason, but this I will not do."

"Then I leave you forever," he cried, rising and quietly leaving the house.

Abbie was in despair. She wrung her hands and wept in anguish. She believed he had gone never to return, and the sun of her life seemed to have set in darkness. Was this to be the end? She, the bride of scarcely a week, a forsaken wife! How terrible an ending to all her bright dreams!

Her mother had heard the sound of their voices, and when the door closed, she hastened to her daughter's room. Abbie sprang up, and, burying her face in her mother's bosom, sobbed out, "O mother, Steve is gone."

"Gone? Gone where?"

"I cannot tell, but he said it was forever."

Mrs. Saunders was shocked, but tried to soothe her by telling her that he could not be in earnest, and would soon return, and trying to draw from her the cause of the trouble. But Abbie felt as though she could not explain, so she said nothing, but continued to weep in silence.

Suddenly the door opened and Rushford stood before them. He paused in astonishment, as he saw Mrs. Saunders, her arms around her daughter. With a low cry of joy, Abbie sprang into his arms. The mother rose, and, looking sternly at him, spoke the single word, "Steven." His eyes fell before her, and she turned and left them alone.

Steven placed his arm tenderly around his young
wife and tried to soothe her. He was deeply morti-
fied that his conduct was known to the mother.
How much Abbie had told her, he did not know.
He knew Mrs. Saunders would not believe him insane, and decided, if anything was said on the subject, to pretend it was a joke. He now felt sure of
Abbie's unquestioning obedience. He had repeat-
edly crossed her will, with always the same result,
silent acquiescence, until now. Still, he could not
help feeling that he had gone just a little too far.
This last trick had better not have been played.
But how confiding his young wife was! He believed that nothing but fear for her life had prevented her from going with him, blindly. Yes, he
could deceive her readily enough, if only he could
the older eyes. With an exultant smile, he pressed
her to his breast, and said soothingly: "Did my
little wife think I could go away and leave her?
My precious little girl! There, do not cry. I could
not live without you. You do not know how much
I love you, or you would not think I could go.
There, there, don't cry. I was only in fun."

These words were intended to soothe her, and
they did, but not in the way he had expected.
They had roused her indignation, for, though she
loved caresses, she did not love to be treated like a
baby. Besides, there was that in his tone which
grated on her feelings, and his words, too, betrayed
the fact that he was perfectly conscious of what had

happened, while she had supposed him to be insane
at the time.   That he was in his right mind now,
she did not doubt.

The truth was he had been so surprised that he
had forgotten his usual caution.   Before he returned
to the house, his plans had been all laid.   He expected to find her ready to ask his forgiveness, and
intended to feign unconsciousness of what had
happened, and surprise at being out of the house.
If she had consented to go, he would have feigned
the return of consciousness before they left the
room.   When she refused to go with him, he had
acted upon the impulse of the moment, not supposing anyone had been awakened.   He had not expected the turn affairs had taken, and was thrown
off his guard.

Abbie was reluctant to believe that he had deceived her, but the fact was self-evident.   Before she
rose from his knees, where in his tenderness he had
drawn her, she was convinced that she had been
deceived.

The family were soon astir, and Steven, gently
kissing her, put her from him and joined the boys
at their work.   Had they known how he had been
employed for the last two hours, his position would
not have been so pleasant.

Though Mrs. Saunders said nothing, Abbie knew
that she was troubled and ill at ease.   She knew
nothing of the tumult in her daughter's breast, for
she had known nothing of her fears.

Poor Abbie! A few hours before she had believed her husband to be insane; this conviction
was forever gone, but in its place was the knowledge
that he had deceived her. Why had he done this?
That he had intended to make her believe that he
was subject to fits of insanity, she could not doubt.
But what was his object? She was sure he must
have some object; she could not believe that a mere
love of torture had actuated him. She remembered that she had never seen any of these symptoms in the presence of others; therefore, it must
be meant for her alone. She determined to watch
him closely, and, by strategy, if necessary, learn his
object.

He believed he had deceived her; he should still
believe so; by no word or act of hers should he
know that she distrusted him.

But, oh, what a position to fill! Scarcely a week
had passed since her wedding night; yet how
changed was everything with her! How bitter her
lot! How dark the future! Her heart must have
failed her entirely, had not the sweet words of her
mother come continually to her mind, "Trust in
God, my child." How sweet those words were to
her! What a privilege to be allowed to trust in that
arm which is mighty to save, even to the uttermost,
those who trust in him! What a comfort now, in
this hour of trouble and disappointment! But for
the sustaining power of the grace of God, she must
have sunk in the pool of despair.

(5)

She had fondly hoped for a life of peace and love. She seemed doomed to a life of disappointment and fear. Now that she had become convinced that she had been purposely deceived, a terrible fear of the future oppressed her. She knew that he was only striving to gain power over her. How would he use that power? What might not happen?

She shuddered to think of it, and, falling upon her knees, she prayed for strength to endure, for wisdom to guide her in fresh trials (for they would come, she felt sure), for courage to face them firmly, and to do her duty unflinchingly.

We believe her prayer was heard and answered, for in all the bitter trials of the next two years, she never once forgot to trust in God.

She looked forward with dread to meeting her husband at the supper hour, but, to her surprise, he was in his pleasantest mood. The men had been chopping a race, and Will, who had been boasting that he could do as much as the best man among them, had 'bushed,' and they were chafing him sorely, while he stoutly protested that they had not given him fair play, and he was not beaten yet.

"Just give me a fair chance," he said, "and I'll show you what a man can do."

"Yes, if he don't happen to bump his nose," said Steve, with a laugh.

"Did Will bump his nose?" asked Roxy, who was always ready for fun.

"Don't it look like it?" asked Steve.

"So it does," said Roxy, staring at him quizzically.

"Does? I should think it did," said Raz. "It looks as red as any toper's."

"And we beat him, too," said Steve, laughing again.

" Indeed you did," said Will. " You didn't give me a fair chance."

"But how did it happen?" asked Roxy, looking eager.

"Well, I'll tell you," said Will. "You know they are always laughing at me because I'm small, and pretend I'm not worth much, though they know very well I'm the smartest man in the crowd. So to-day I got tired of their nonsense, and challenged them for a race.

"I could see they were a little afraid to tackle me, but they were ashamed to say so, and, choosing two logs of near the same size, Raz and Elton took one, and Steve and I took the other. We began all fair enough, but just as I got mine about half off, Steve, who couldn't help seeing that I was beating him all to nothing, managed to roll the log. Well, you see, I wasn't looking for that, and somehow my nose came in sudden contact with the ground. I felt somewhat astonished, I can tell you. Before I could make it all out, and get back to work, they were done. Now I'll leave it to the crowd if that was a fair beat."

All laughed heartily at Will's description of his mishap.   Many jokes followed, and the supper hour passed pleasantly away.

When they had finished their meal, Will said they had fairly beaten him at the table, if they had not in the timber.

" Will feels so bad because we beat him that he couldn't eat half enough," laughed Steve.

"He will have to have a piece," chimed in Raz.

"Yes, he'll be going to the cupboard before night," said Steve.

"If I do, I wo't lock the kitchen door, " said Will, winking at Abbie.

A laugh followed this sally, and Joe said he guessed Steve "was glad he didn't say nothing."

Some time passed, and nothing more happened to arouse Abbie's fears.   She began to hope that she had been needlessly alarmed, and grew cheerful and happy again.

Mr. Saunders returned, and, seeing her appear so happy, began to be more reconciled to the match.

CHAPTER VI.

BOUT this time Mr. Elton, who had occupied the shanty on the Erastus claim, began to talk of returning to his friends in Illinois, for, as his wife did not like the country, he had decided not to take land, but return and find a home near her family, which he soon did, leaving the house empty.

It was soon arranged that Abbie and Steve were to occupy it. Here Abbie had her first experience in housekeeping. Her house consisted of only one room, ten by twelve feet, built of logs, and with a board roof. A small bedstead filled one corner of the room, and a stove another, while a homemade basswood table stood against one side of the room. Above it were three shelves, which comprised her cupboard. Two chairs completed the furniture of her new home, yet there she spent the happiest days of her married life.

Her husband was now all that she could wish. He was very kind and attentive, and during the long winter evenings he spent many a pleasant hour fashioning some useful article of furniture, until Abbie playfully remarked that they would

(69)

have to have a larger house, as this would not hold them all.

Her brothers and sisters often came to visit them, testing the ingenuity of the young hostess to seat them comfortably. This would be accomplished at last by the ladies taking the bed for a sofa, while Abbie's trunk was drawn out to serve for another. When all were seated, jokes were cracked, for want of nuts. The boys said the corn popped as well as though they all had chairs, and all were as happy as if in a palace.

The winter passed away. Spring brought plenty of work on the new farm, and Steve was again employed by Mr. Saunders, for he still showed no inclination to take land of his own, but depended wholly upon his father-in-law for support. As might be supposed, Mr. Saunders did not like this state of affairs. If Steve had shown himself determined to make a home for his young wife, he would willingly have given them their living until they should be able to raise their own. This, however, Steve showed no intention of doing, and he was obliged to submit for his daughter's sake.

Abbie, too, was not pleased, but as her husband had been very kind to her, and as the unpleasant symptoms of the first week of her marriage seemed to have entirely passed away, she strove to conquer all unpleasant reflections, and do her part toward making home happy. She fully believed the words of the Saviour, " Enter into thy closet, and when thou hast shut thy door, pray to thy Father which is in secret; and thy Father which seeth in secret shall reward thee openly." They seemed to have been written expressly for her, and their truth was daily verified to her. It had become her daily custom to kneel in secret, just before her husband returned from the field, and ask the blessing of her Father upon their interview, and to teach her her duty, so that, if possible, she might gain her husband's love to that extent that all unpleasantness might pass away.

Suddenly, one evening, just as they were about to retire for the night, Steve's face assumed that strange, wild look. He sprang to the side of his wife, and, as if in mortal terror, clung to her, looking toward the closed door, and shrinking behind her, as if to escape some terrible object.

The farce was well played, but Abbie was not deceived, although she was frightened. It had come so suddenly, when she had felt so secure. Her first thought was to upbraid him; but she hoped, by allowing the farce, to find out the object he had in view. So she soothed him as best she could, asking what had frightened him.

He would not answer, but continued by every act to evince fear of something from the door. She tried to persuade him to go to bed, and at last succeeded; but just as he was about to lay his head on the pillow, he sprang up, looked eagerly at the door, then sprang swiftly through it. In an instant

he was back, bearing the ax, which he placed at
the head of the bed, then retired with a satisfied air.

This last act startled her more than anything
else had done. What could he want of the ax?
Did he mean to kill her? A shudder passed
through her frame at the thought. No; she would
not believe it. Again from her heart there rose a
silent prayer to God for strength to bear this new
trial.

Steve lay covertly watching her as she disrobed,
feeling both angry and surprised at her undisturbed manner. He could not know the terrible
tumult in her breast, or how fervently she had
prayed to be delivered from further trial; nor could
he know how firm was her faith in God, or the wild
prayer that was then rising to heaven that she
might yet gain her husband's love. He did not
know that this distrust of him, this knowledge that
he loved to play with her fears, was a greater trial
to this gentle, trusting heart than bodily harm
could be. He only felt that she was not deceived,
that she must despise him, and anger and mortification suggested revenge.

From that day he seemed to be constantly trying to vex her. Little things were done that he
knew she did not like; yet he still professed great
love for her. She would pass them by without a
word; she knew he did those things to torment
her, and she tried hard not to notice them. Her
very silence seemed to vex him, yet, if she spoke

to him in the most gentle entreaty, he would become very angry, accusing her of making a great fuss, and trying to make people believe he was a terribly bad fellow, although he knew she never spoke of the matter in the presence of others.

The summer passed. The grain was harvested, and preparations were made for winter. Mr. Saunders had built a new house on his place, and Steve and Abbie moved into the old one vacated by him. The large, roomy apartment was a pleasant change from the one in which Abbie had taken her first lessons in housekeeping. And now she had to take another lesson in this important branch of labor,—the arranging of her homemade furniture to the best advantage.

This was a pleasant occupation to her. When all was done that she could do to make home happy, and the evening meal was spread, she sat down by the fire, over which the kettle was singing cheerily, and looked about her. She felt for a moment as if she could be happy; then, as she thought of her husband, a feeling of despair began to creep into her heart.

Winter came on. But for her friends she would have suffered much from neglect. She was confined to the house, and, as her mother could not see her often on account of sickness at home, she felt quite forsaken. But "Trust in God" was still her motto. Indeed, she had need to trust—scarcely one year married, yet only the wreck of her former self! One short year ago she was happy and free, now—must we say it?—an unloved wife, doomed to terrible torture from him who had promised at the altar to love, cherish, and protect her.

Oh, how fervently she prayed for the love of her husband! How she dreaded his approach, yet how she longed for his love! There had been a time when she feared she should learn to hate him. Now, for her sake—for the sake of her unborn babe—she prayed for his love. She felt that she could forgive him freely for all the pain that he had caused her if he would only love her again, and she prayed for strength to bear her suffering patiently.

She had need of strength. Her husband returned at night in a towering passion with her father. He had offended him in some way, and words could not express his anger. He completely exhausted himself in pouring out abusive words, declaring he would kill him before he slept. The trembling wife dared not utter a word, even to ask the cause of his anger, but she gathered from his words that he hated the old curmudgeon, that he had been trying some time to pick a quarrel, but the old hypocrite pretended to be too pious, and treated him for all the world like a puppy; he would make him speak—so he would—or he would break his old head for him.

"I'll kill him before I sleep," he cried, rising and rushing out.

Abbie was more frightened now than she had
ever been for herself. She hardly dared move until he was gone; then, throwing herself upon the
bed, she wept until she could weep no more. In
imagination she saw her father slain by her husband's hand. The picture was a fearful one! She
buried her face in her pillow to shut out the horrible scene.

She lay, trembling and exhausted, until she heard
footsteps approach the door. Her husband entered quietly, and, seeing that she had retired,
stealthily approached the bed. Leaning over, he
peered into her face. She closed her eyes, and
dared not move, lest his anger be turned upon her.
Satisfying himself that she slept, he went quietly
to bed, and was soon snoring loudly. Abbie was
much exhausted, and soon fell asleep.

O gentle sleep, thou great restorer of exhausted
nature, what a blessing thou art to poor mortals,
while struggling through this vale of tears!

CHAPTER VII.

THE BIRTH OF LITTLE ELLA.

AYS pass, and we again enter the home of our heroine. Everything is quiet and in order. A bright fire burns in the stove. A chair sits beside it, on which rests the family cat, purring gently to herself. At first the room seems deserted; soon a sound attracts our attention; we turn, and on a bed in the corner of the room lies the young wife.

She is very pale and thin; hard lines are drawn around her mouth; on her forehead sad marks of pain and sorrow are plainly visible. She is asleep, but soon a nestling sound is heard, then a tiny voice, and the young mother wakes with a start. Hearing the voice at her side, a sweet and holy light comes into her listless eyes, while she gently raises the little form, and, clasping it in her arms, tries to soothe it with tender, loving words.

It was a sad but beautiful sight. The pale young mother, with her large black eyes, seeming ever to remind you of a life of sorrow and suffering, with her pallid cheek resting on the snow-white pillow; the babe, scarce a week old, whose cheek she has

(76)

placed lovingly upon her own, gazing with its large, wondering blue eyes at whatever object they chanced to meet, made a picture for a painter.

They were alone. Neighbors were scarce, as is often the case in a new country, and a nurse could not be found. Mrs. Saunders was obliged to divide her time between her daughter and her own family. She had been there several hours, and made them as comfortable as possible. She was then obliged to return home, and had left her daughter in the care of her husband. Soon after she left, Mr. Rushford had risen, stepped to the door, looked out, then turned to his wife, saying, "I guess I'll step over to the post office a minute."

Abbie started in surprise. It was two miles to the post office, and she knew he could not return in less than two hours, as the ground was covered with snow, and scarcely any road. She was not able to rise from her bed. Her mother had gone home, supposing she was in good care, and probably would not call again until evening. What might not happen to her and her darling while he was away? She knew it was useless to ask him to stay, but fear lent her courage, and she said timidly:—

"Please do not stay long. I shall be so lonely."

"Oh, you will be all right!" he answered carelessly.

"But the fire will be all out," she urged, almost hoping to persuade him to stay.

"I will build one now," he said, going to the stove and filling it with wood. "There, now you will be all right."

"But suppose baby should cry?" making one more effort to detain him.

"Still her, then," was the heartless answer, as he went out and closed the door.

Abbie looked anxiously at the clock. It was half past two. He would be back by half past four. For some time she lay quietly watching the fire as it crackled and blazed, throwing out a genial warmth. The cat came soberly up and climbed into a chair to enjoy it.

How cozy and quiet it seemed! Baby still slept sweetly. Perhaps it would sleep until its father returned. She nestled closer to the pillow, and fell asleep. She slept soundly until roused by the low wail of her babe. She succeeded in quieting it for a few minutes, as we have seen, but not for long. It soon began to clamor for food, which she could not give it without assistacce. The fire was out, and the room was as cold as a winter day could make it.

She could not even rise in bed without danger to herself. Baby's cries grew louder and more violent. She must do something. She feebly rose to a sitting posture, and strove to still the child with its natural food. But she was weak, nervous, and inexperienced, and the babe continued to cry. Oh, if she could only get to the fire! She was almost fainting with cold and weariness, when the door opened, and her husband appeared. A look of relief came over her face, quickly followed by one of fear and anxiety. Her husband glanced around the room, then bade her lie down. She obeyed, not daring to refuse.

He strode to the stove, built a fire, then, coming to the bed, took the child, which was still crying, roughly from its mother's arms, went to the stove, and sat down moodily, doing nothing to quiet the child. The babe soon cried itself to sleep, when it was returned to the mother, with the remark, "There, I guess it's done now."

Abbie clasped it to her breast, which was just then filled with such a mixture of emotions as it is impossible to describe. Would she ever forget that hour? Yet her cup of woe was hardly tasted. Baby slept the sleep of utter exhaustion. Abbie received her supper from the hands of her husband, and ate it in silence. Will called in the evening to say that mother could not come until morning.

Soon baby woke, and again cried for food. Abbie rose to supply it, but before it was satisfied, her husband ordered her to lie down. She begged for a few minutes more, which angered him, and, snatching the child from her arms, he again ordered her to lie down.

She obeyed, trembling with fear for the child. He took it in his arms, and repeated the operation of the afternoon. Three times did it cry, until it had to stop from sheer exhaustion, its little voice growing weaker and weaker, until it could make no sound. Then the father gave it back to the trembling mother, with the heartless remark: "There, she's quiet now. Give her some dinner."

But the poor babe was so exhausted that it could take no nourishment, and Abbie feared for its life. It lay like one dead, scarcely breathing. Oh, what anguish filled the mother's heart at this moment! Alas, pen cannot describe it! If she could only take it to the fire! But she could not. She dared do nothing but clasp it to her aching breast, while the father slept, or seemed to sleep, as if nothing had happened. But she was too frightened to sleep. What should she do, what could she do, to avert the danger she felt threatened her darling! For herself she did not care. She could bear until death released her from her suffering.

Was it not her duty to make known her situation to her friends, and solicit their protection, for her babe's sake, if not for her own? She knew that, if she would tell her story and leave her cruel husband, they would welcome her home, and protect her with their lives. This was a dreadful alternative, and she could not conclude to adopt it. Weary and exhausted, she at last fell asleep.

Just as the day began to dawn, Mr. Rushford rose, dressed himself, and turned to look at his wife. Her face was plainly revealed, as she lay all unconscious of his gaze. How pale and thin she looked!

Could it be death? No, no, not that! He shuddered at the thought, and tried to turn away, but he
could not. Again his gaze was fastened upon her.
He saw the infant clasped tenderly in her arms.
She seemed trying to protect it while she slept.
There were traces of tears on her face. The babe
nestled in her bosom; she moved uneasily and a
sigh escaped her. Opening her eyes, she saw his
gaze fixed upon her. Fear held her quiet, while he,
starting like some guilty thing, turned and busied
himself about the fire.

That scene had stirred up some remaining spark
of humanity, and a feeling of remorse came over
him. He called himself a villain, and resolved to
reform. He went back to their first acquaintance,
and remembered how his interest in his pale young
wife had been first awakened, not by any arts of
hers to attract him, but by her patient and unre-
mitting attention to duty.

He remembered his first deception, and his un-
reasonable thirst for revenge on her for her fancied
coldness; how he had remained in the family, pretending great love for his mother's old friend; how
he had pressed his claims to her hand at the first
opportunity; how he had hastened the wedding
day, lest something might happen to open their
eyes and thwart his plans; how impatient he had
been to be sure she was all his own; how soon he
had commenced his system of revenge!

He knew that she bore on her person, at that

6

moment, many a mark of his cruelty, though he
had taken care that they should be well concealed.
Now that conscience had been allowed to speak,
she accused him unmercifully. A strong desire to
confess his fault took possession of him, but he
feared he should then lose his power over her. No,
he would not do that. He would be kind to her
and the child. That would be sufficient. There
was no need to humiliate himself. He rose and
approached the bed.

Abbie, who had been watching him, not daring
to speak, was surprised and pleased to see a look
of tenderness in his face. When he spoke pleasantly to her, a flush of joy overspread her face, and
she was ready to forget all his former unkindness.

"How is my little wife this morning?" he asked,
in tones as strange as they were sweet.

"Much better," she replied, almost believing, for
a moment, her troubles forever past.

"I am so glad," he said. "Do you think you
could be helped to your chair? It would seem so
pleasant to see you up again."

Abbie was so happy she could hardly speak,
but she faltered out, "Mother will be here soon,
and we can ask her."

"Just as you please," he said. "Perhaps it will
be best to wait. In the meantime, I will get our
breakfast."

He bustled about with a cheerful air, putting
things to rights, and preparing for breakfast with

an alacrity that was truly surprising. Abbie took
the meal from his hands with feelings of thankfulness and wonder. She had prayed so fervently for
his love. Could it be that her prayer was answered?

Mrs. Saunders soon came in, shaking the snow
from her garments.

"How do you all do this morning?" she asked,

"Nicely," said Steve. "Abbie is better, and we
have been talking of getting her up."

"You do indeed look better," she said, looking
at Abbie. "There is quite a flush on your cheek."
Then, turning to Steve, she added, "I think she
may get up a little while."

Steve seemed pleased, and stood ready to do all
he could. Abbie, still wondering at his altered
appearance, gladly accepted his assistance. She
did not know that he feared, every time her mother
came near her, that she might discover those un-
lucky scars, and find out that they were made by
his hand. When she had been placed in a comfortable position, he felt safer, and sat down by the
stove.

Mrs. Saunders took up the babe, and soon noticed that all was not right.

"Why, Abbie, baby is sick!" she exclaimed,
as the limp little form lay "like a rag," she said,
upon her lap.

Abbie bent over it in alarm. She had feared as
much. Steve started from his chair, and came to

look at the child. Its face was pale, and wore a
pinched expression, while it seemed too weak to
move. They began to remove the wraps. Mrs.
Saunders uttered an exclamation of alarm.

"What is it? Oh! what is the matter?" cried
Abbie.

"Has she been crying much?" asked her mother.

"Yes," said Abbie, then stopped in confusion.

Mrs. Saunders quickly undressed the child, and
found it slowly bleeding to death. Hurriedly she
changed the bandages and stopped the bleeding.
After administering a restorative, she asked Abbie
how it had happened.

It was a trying moment. Abbie was weeping at
the danger of the child. She thought of the cause,
and indignation filled her heart. She longed to
tell her mother the whole story. Then she remembered his kindness of the morning, and decided to shield him, hoping he would really reform.
So she said: "Steve had to go out, and I was
alone a short time. She woke and I could not
still her. Steve came in and took her, but she
cried until she fell asleep."

Steve breathed a sigh of relief. She had covered up his infamous act, if she had not lied. Not
one word had been said of the walk to the post
office, not one word that would imply that he had
been gone more than a few minutes.

Mrs. Saunders accepted the explanation, but told
her there was great danger that the child would

not live.   Turning to Steve, she asked him to go
and tell her family that she could not come at
present, and sat down to watch the little sufferer.
Abbie was again put to bed by Steve, who had not
been long absent, and who did not again leave the
room while Mrs. Saunders remained.

He was afraid Abbie might conclude to tell her
mother all that had happened. He need not have
feared.   Once she had decided to screen him, nothing could have induced her to disclose her secret.

Mrs. Saunders was both grieved and angry at
what had happened. She knew Abbie had kept
back something, and, though she did not imagine
the truth, she felt sure the child had not been well
cared for, and she decided to be more watchful in
the future.

But her duties at home would prevent her from
remaining with them, so she must see if something
could not be done. Steve seemed to be unconscious of the danger of the child, and she felt that its
safety, or that of its mother, must not be intrusted
to his care.   She racked her brain to think of someone who might come, but she could not think of
one who had not been called upon, and gave up in
despair, saying she must send Roxy, though how
she could spare her she did not see.

Abbie had noticed a change in her husband
within the last few hours. When the illness of the
babe had been discovered, he had evinced such
strong emotion that Abbie hoped it would be a

lasting lesson. He turned pale and did not speak,
but when she was questioned, he gave her such a
beseeching look that she could not expose his conduct to her mother. It could not benefit the child,
and might do harm, she had argued. When she
had told her story, shielding him from blame, he
felt such a sense of relief that he could have thanked
her heartily, yet he could not but fear that she
might yet say something that would attach blame
to him.

As time passed, and the babe seemed to revive,
and nothing more was said to arouse his fears for
himself, he became exultant, believing she dared
not tell, and he was safe. His manner had changed,
and Abbie grew more and more uneasy. She was
glad her sister was coming, but she felt she would
be little protection.

Roxy came, and for several days there was nothing especial to trouble her mind. The babe im-
proved, she felt her strength returning, and looked
forward with pleasure to the time when she could
resume her usual duties. Her husband, though
not as attentive as at first, was not really unkind,
and, relieved from actual torture, she felt she could
endure to the end. Again hope returned to
brighten her path, so full of sadness.

Alas, her cup of sorrow was scarcely tasted, and
she was doomed to drain it to the very dregs!
Her careful concealment of her husband's misdeeds
had emboldened him, and he was, even now, con-
templating other acts of cruelty.

The room was so pleasant, and had such an air
of comfort this morning. Roxy, though but four-
teen years old, was spry and active, and everything
in the poor, plain room was as neat as she could
make it. A bright fire gave out a genial warmth.
Abbie sat near it, looking pale and thin, with her
babe on her knee. As she gazed upon its little
face, a smile lighted up her own.

Roxy bent over the little form, saying, "Oh,
isn't she sweet, Abbie!"

The mother answered with a look of fond pride.

"She will look so pretty when she learns to
laugh," said Roxy.

"She looks pretty now," said the fond mother,
to whom the babe on her lap was the perfection of
beauty.

The little red face, with its blue, wondering eyes,
the nose, the mouth, the chin, even the thin, color-
less hair, which seemed striving to cover the little
round head, was a marvel of beauty to her.

What a cozy picture they made—the pale young
mother, the infant on her knee, and the still younger
auntie bending over it with fond pride!

Alas, that it should be so rudely disturbed!
They started, as footsteps were heard at the door.
The latch was raised, and Steve entered with a
swagger, and sat down near them. He looked at
them with an insolent leer, took out a roll of to-
bacco, and, taking a large mouthful, rolled it into
one cheek, then, looking around him with a comic
air, he said:—

"Well, now, this is comfortable! Here I've got a wife, a baby," emphasizing the words in the most disagreeable manner, "and a little girl to wait on them. How happy I ought to be!" He waited for some reply, but neither deigned to speak. His manner, more than his words, was displeasing to them. "Say, wife," he continued, "don't you think I ought to be happy?"

"I do, indeed," feeling that she must say something. There was a touching pathos in her voice, and a strange earnestness in her look as she said this, but he did not heed it.

"So do I," said he; "this is charming. Here's Abbie, looking as old and motherly as need be—why, she don't look no more like she did a year ago than nothing, and she can just thank me for it all," with a grimace which did not hide his wicked smile. "I've just made her what she is. Haven't I, wife?"

"You have, indeed," she answered bitterly, her heart swelling with indignation, as she thought of his cold-blooded cruelty.

Roxy looked on in surprise and wonder. She knew nothing of Abbie's trials and suffering, and of course could not realize how cruel his remarks really were. She had never thought much of her brother-in-law, but she did not know he was actually cruel.

He felt the bitterness in her tone, and exulted in the pain he was giving. "Of course I have," he said. "If it had not been for my judicious treatment you might have looked as rosy and green now as you did, when Charley saw you last," and he looked at her keenly to note the effect of his words. The effect was greater than he had expected. She had felt his cruel thrusts deeply—how deeply he could never know. When he had spoken that name, every vestige of color had left her face, and she sank back like one dead.

He was startled, and, coming to her, took her in his arms and laid her on the bed. He was very tender and arranged the bedclothing with care, then, placing the babe in her arms, he stood off and contemplated the picture.

His trepidation had lasted only while he thought her fainting. As he looked at her as she lay, a little paler, perhaps, than usual, with her eyes fixed on his face as if she would read his very heart, he almost relented. But, smothering the feeling of shame that came over him, he said: "I wonder how he would like that picture? I hardly think he would know you."

She made no sign, spoke no word, but continued to gaze at him. He flinched before her gaze, and, turning on his heel with a coarse attempt at a laugh, sat down by the stove. He was silent for a few moments, then began such a scene as pen cannot describe.

He would taunt Roxy, saying everything he could to vex her, then he would break out with a snatch of some rude song, then, turning to his wife, he would ask with mock solicitude how she felt. Receiving no answer, save the gaze of those eyes which had troubled him, he would laugh aloud. He seemed perfectly reckless, never pausing, but going from one thing to another with perfect heartlessness.

Once he asked her what she would do if he should commit some terrible crime. She did not answer until forced to, then said she did not know." Poor thing! she did not know. She only knew that the terrible truth had been forced home to her heart that there was not one spark of love in her husband's heart for her; that he had married her only for revenge. She felt that his future pleasure lay in torturing her. That he was expedient in devising means of torture, she had learned to her cost.

She tried to picture to herself what her future life must be, but her brain refused to work. She longed to fly from all this misery, but she could do nothing. She settled into a cold, calm state of apathy, seeming to wait, wait—she knew not for what.

CHAPTER VIII.

FURTHER CRUELTIES.

STEVE RUSHFORD looked at his wife keenly for a moment, and then said: "Don't know? Begin to think, then, for I don't know what I shall do. Oh, yes, I think I do! I think I'll take you down to my mother's. She'll help me train you. I haven't half a chance here. 'Fraid of your folks, you see. They might interfere with me here. There'll be no danger there, and if I want any help, there is plenty to lend a hand. Will you go?"

"I suppose so," she said mechanically, for it did not occur to her that she could do otherwise if he chose to take her there.

He elevated his eyebrows in surprise, evidently expecting a different answer, then went on: "All right. But you can say 'good-by' to your folks, for you'll never see them again." He paused for a response, but, receiving none, continued: "I don't mean you shall have anything more to do with any of them. They make you so ugly I can't live with you."

He knew this was false, but he was becoming angry because she would not talk' and thought to force her to retort. But she did not answer, and he went on, repeating that he meant to take her entirely away from all the Saunderses; but, on second thought, he would not take her to his mother, for she might take it into her head to pity the daughter of her old friend; he would go away into the wilderness somewhere; he did not need help; he could manage her himself, once he got her away from her folks.

He liked the plan better, as he went on, and concluded to start next week. She would be well enough by that time, and as he was determined to go, the sooner it was over the better. He expected her "dad" would make a great fuss, but he could soon "settle him." If there was one Saunders less in the world when he left, so much the better for the world. Abbie need not take any pains to fix up, for she would likely not live to get there' anyway. Perhaps he better not take her, it would only be trouble for nothing, and he hated the whole Saunders race.

Of course he must take his baby. He couldn't be expected to go without his baby, all the baby he had in the world. Yes, he would take it along. His mother could take care of it. He would never leave it there to be brought up among the Saunderses.

At the mention of taking the child, the young mother started, partly rose, and appeared to be going to speak, then dropped back on her pillow. He saw this move, and his eyes flashed with demoniac pleasure. He had made her feel at last, and with renewed vigor he continued.

He pictured the grief of the little one, as it was taken from its worthless mother; the cold and hunger it might be expected to suffer; but, if it lived to get there, his mother would take good care of it, and bring it up decently. He should take good care that it was taught to hate its mother, and all her relatives.

All this and much more he said, stopping to note the effect of each cruel speech. He was surprised at her passive coldness. Only once had she evinced any feeling, and then only for a moment. He feared he was losing all his power over her.

Alas, the heart was frozen with grief! While she followed him with her eyes, scarcely turning them away, she would not have raised a hand if he had placed a knife to her throat.

Exasperated at not being enabled to elicit any show of grief, he rose and walked up and down the room, coming near her head and talking in a different strain. His tone was low and fierce. He said it would be much better if she were dead. Then she would not care what became of the babe. Stopping suddenly, he took from a sack which contained tools, a file. It was a large one, such as are used for filing plows, and had no handle, leaving the sharp end of the iron bare.

He threw it with such force against the wall near her head that it entered the wood sufficiently to hold its weight, and then stepped back to see the effect. She started a little, that was all, but kept her eyes fastened upon him. Again and again was the experiment repeated. As he grew more expert, he ventured nearer and nearer, until the disengaged end nearly touched her head. But she never moved a muscle. Fear held her like a vise. When at last, wearied out by the exertion, he was obliged to stop and turn to something else, she could not have told how long the drama had lasted.

All day long had it continued. A fearful snowstorm had begun about noon, and there was no fear of being disturbed, as all were glad to keep close to their own fire. All day long the snow continued to fall, as if it would never stop; and all day and far into the night did the fearful storm within continue to fall on the head of the defenseless woman.

Roxy, trembling with fear, crept off to bed. At length tired nature gave way and Abbie slept the dreamless sleep of utter exhaustion. Again we repeat, blessed angel of sleep! How often she comes to save from utter madness!

Long and heavily did she sleep. When she awoke, her husband was by her side. She shuddered at his touch. Oh! why could she not have slept forever? Why must she still live and act out this terrible drama? Life was not worth the pain it cost. Oh, was there no way to escape from this terrible thralldom!

As if divining her thoughts, her husband said, "Well, what do you calculate to do?"

The question was so sudden that she could not answer. What could she do? She could not tell.

"I thought," he continued calmly, "that you might conclude to go home. Of course we cannot live together after this. You can take what little we have in the house. It was all yours at first, so you can take it."

What disinterested kindness (?)! But Abbie did not think of this. She was waiting to hear what he would say of the child.

"Then you can have all your own clothes, and the baby's, for I have concluded to let you keep her for me for a short time—say until she is a year old.

Abbie's heart gave a great bound and seemed to fill her throat to suffocation. This was what she had been longing to hear, for she had determined to escape if possible. She was too overjoyed to move or speak, and he continued:—

"If you want to go, I will hitch up the team and take you. I shall keep the team, of course, for, although they were given to you, I think they belong to me now."

Abbie had nothing to say to this. If he would only let her have her child (in her ignorance she thought he could take it from her at any moment), peaceably, she would ask no more. Fearing he might change his mind, she rose and began hurriedly to dress.

"Are you going?" he asked. "If so, I must get up and harness the team."

"Yes."

That single word was all she could speak. She was trembling with fear and excitement. He did not seem to notice this, but went out to feed the team.

As Abbie glanced from the window, she saw that it was break of day and the sky was clear. But she had no time to pause. She must be doing. Now that she had decided to go, she was in feverish haste to be there. When she was at home by the dear old hearth, with father, mother, brothers, and sisters around her, she would feel safe, but not before. Roxy was up and a bright fire burned in the stove. Abbie sat down before it and carefully dressed the babe, imprinting many kisses on its unconscious face and tiny fists, while Roxy looked on in wonder. She had heard what had been said, but had not uttered a word. She knew in a vague way that her sister was going home, but could not comprehend the full meaning of the words. Could her sister? We shall see.

Steve came in smiling, and asked her if she was ready.

"Not quite," she answered; "I haven't packed all of baby's clothes yet."

"Let me take her while you finish," he said, with an amused smile. "I will hold her carefully."

There was something in his tone and look that surprised and terrified the young mother. What meant that merry twinkle in his eye, that amused look on his face? What was there to laugh at, at such a time as this, when, perhaps, he was taking his child in his arms for the last time for many months, perhaps forever? Could she trust him? Would he give her back her darling?

She hesitated, then turned to her sister. Seeing this, he quickly stepped between them, pushing Roxy to one side, and roughly took the child from its mother's arms, while such a look of anger overspread his face that Abbie's heart stood still with fear. But, remembering that she was still in his power, and dependent on him for help to escape, she controlled herself, and turned to complete her preparations for departure.

Rushford sat down with the child, and watched her as she passed to and fro, getting one article after another together. She had not noticed him since turning away from that look, but seemed absorbed in her work.

He saw her close the trunk, and heard the click of the lock as it turned and shot home, thus securing the contents. The key was carefully put in her pocket, then she brought out baby's trunk. Its cloak and hood were taken out and laid on the bed beside her own. Then the discarded clothes were put in, and this lock also shot home with a click.

It sounded ominous, and he turned suddenly and bowed his head over the child, prepared to put a stop to this farce. He had not expected her to take up with his offer, but when she did, he thought he would teach her a lesson she would not soon

7

forget. He told her the team was ready, when they were standing in their stalls, munching their oats, without a thought of being taken out. She had believed him, but it was time she should know the truth.

His busy brain suggested a plan for bringing her to terms if she proved determined. As she approached him, equipped for her ride, with baby's cloak and hood in her hand, she was surprised to see his head bowed over the child and his burly form shaking as if with mighty sobs, and to hear his voice, seemingly choked with emotion, saying, "O my baby!"

She was touched at the sight, never doubting that it was genuine grief. She had wondered if he could let it go from him without one endearing word, without one kiss on its velvet cheek. So she waited patiently for his emotion to subside.

"O my baby!" he said. "O my precious darling! How can papa live without you! O Abbie!" he cried, looking up into her face for the first time. To her surprise she saw that his eyes were perfectly dry, though he had appeared to be shedding oceans of tears, while his face wore a comical look of mock anguish.) "O Abbie! how can I let her go? Why will you take her away from her poor father?"

Abbie grew uneasy as she looked into his eyes, and made an attempt to take the child, but he held her fast.

"Oh, give her to me, please!" cried Abbie, a dreadful fear seizing her heart.

"No," he said, straightening up, and assuming a look of firmness. "No, you shall not take her from me. I love my child too well to part with her. If you do not, you can go, but she stays with me."

Abbie stood as if turned to stone. She could neither move nor speak. She turned deadly pale, but her husband was calm and collected. He was getting used to these scared looks, but, fearing she might fall, he drew a chair near him, and told her to sit down. She obeyed mechanically. A dread faintness came over her. She wondered if she was going to faint. But thoughts of her child came to her, and, making a mighty effort to calm herself, she held out her arms, mutely, for the child.

"Not just yet," he said, fastening his cold, gleaming eyes on her face pitilessly. "I wish to talk to you first. Before I trust my precious babe with you, you must promise to be very tender with her."

"Oh, yes!" cried she. "I promise with all my heart. Oh, give her to me!" again holding out her arms appealingly.

"Not quite so fast," he said, still trying to hold her with his baleful eyes. "Not quite so fast. Do you know what you are about to do?"

"I think I do," she replied more firmly, for she had seemed to hear her mother's voice saying, "Trust in God, my child," and the thought gave her new strength. She no longer feared and trembled, but there came into her heart a calm assurance of faith that God would indeed be a present help in time of need.

He noticed her changed manner, and, fearing he was again losing his power, he continued, in more persuasive tones: "You think you do? Well, I think you do not. You propose to take my child under the roof of the man I hate with a terrible hatred, and who, I believe, hates me. You must promise not to let him teach my child to hate me."

Abbie thought how much cause her father had to hate him, but, knowing him too well to think he would do such a thing, readily gave her promise.

"Now," said he, "you must promise to let me have her whenever I call for her."

This was a trying moment for poor Abbie. She was flying from the man who had nearly taken the life of her child, yet she must give her promise to surrender it on demand. She believed that he could take it at any time by the laws of the land. All she could do was to "trust in God" for the rest, after getting possession of the babe.

"I promise," she said.

He looked at her a moment, then at the babe, which was quietly sleeping, all unconscious of the drama that was being played over it or of the part it played.

He leaned over it in mock tenderness, saying: "O my babe, my sweet, precious babe! How can I let you go!" Then, springing up excitedly, he exclaimed: "I cannot, I will not let her go!

Either you must stay with me or leave your child."

Abbie's face had grown cold and hard. She knew that he had been playing with her feelings, and her heart swelled with indignation. Springing up, she caught his arm, and said, in a voice low and trembling: "This farce must stop. Give me the babe."

He looked in her face a moment, and, seeing something he could not understand, handed her the child. As Abbie took the child, a feeling of exultation came over her. But when she remembered that she was still in his power, and that, although she was determined to escape, she could not do so without his aid unless she could send word to her friends—and what might not happen before she could do this!—she sat down with the child in her arms and burst into tears.

But we must leave them for a few moments and follow the footsteps of Roxy, who, at Steve's first refusal to deliver the child to its mother, had quietly left the room, unnoticed by either of its occupants.

CHAPTER IX.

ABBIE RESCUED FROM DANGER.

S soon as Roxy found herself outside the door, she flew as fast as her feet could carry her toward home. But the snow was deep, there was no road, the air was bitter cold, and before she had accomplished half the distance, she was almost ready to drop with fatigue. But she toiled bravely on, in spite of the cold and the snow, until she reached the door, which she opened and rushed wildly in, crying, "O father, come quick!"

Mr. Saunders sat by the fire with his children around him, and one little one upon his knee. Mrs. Saunders was busy about her household duties. Neither dreamed of danger until Roxy's sudden appearance startled them. All was instantly confusion.

"What is the matter, child?" cried Mrs. Saunders. "Why are you so frightened? What has happened?"

Roxy, entirely overcome by fright and fatigue, had dropped into the nearest chair, and, covering her face with her hands, began weeping violently. It was some time before she could control herself sufficiently to answer them at all, and even then she

(102)

was too excited to give them a clear understanding
of the matter.   But they gathered this at last, that
"Steve was acting up so awful they could not live
with him.   He wouldn't let Abbie have the baby.
He had 'most killed her and father must come
quick!"

Consternation seized them both at this intelligence.   Abbie was in danger, and they must rescue
her at all hazards.   But how was the question.
The boys had all gone to the woods for their day's
work and Mr. Saunders was alone.   Could he, in
his age and infirmity, hope to cope with the strong,
burly form of Steve, who, he feared, by his daughter's story, was furious?   He might even now be
killing her.   He sprang up at the thought and
began hurriedly to don his outdoor garments, when
his wife laid a restraining hand on his arm.

"Do not detain me," he said.   "I must go to
her."

"I would not detain you, but you must not go
alone."

"But how can it be avoided?   Help she must
have immediately, and the boys are all away.   No,
I must go alone."

Suiting the action to the word, he started for the
door.   But Mrs. Saunders feared the consequences
should he go alone, and her busy brain suggested
a plan ere he reached it.

"Go for Mr. Deering," she said.   "He will go
with you, and you may need his help."

"So I will," he replied as he closed the door after him.

Roxy had become quiet by this time, and Mrs. Saunders, fearing that Steve might notice her absence and mistrust where she had gone, persuaded her to return, and, if possible, not let him know that she had been away. Being assured that her father would soon be there, she returned and quietly entered the room.

Abbie sat weeping, with her babe in her arms, while Steve was laying down rules by which she was to be guided in the future. He had never intended to allow her to leave the house, had played his part merely for pleasure, and to see how far she would go, that he might have something to taunt her with.

He little guessed the power of will that lay in that timid, shrinking heart. He could no more hold her now than he could stop the whirlwind in its course. She was even then determining, with her sister's help, to effect her escape. Nor did he guess how near her escape was.

He had grown secure in his mind, as he saw her weeping (she saw the folly of trying to escape him, he thought), and was laying down his rules with great emphasis, when footsteps were heard approaching the house. Roxy gave a sigh of relief. Steve had just time to assume a careless air, when Mr. Saunders entered, followed by Mr. Deering.

As Abbie caught sight of her father, her heart
gave a great bound, then seemed to stand still with
the excess of her joy. "Saved, saved at last!" she
cried, stretching out her arms appealingly toward
him. She did not heed the presence of Mr. Deering, but thought only of safety for herself and babe.

Mr. Saunders stood a moment, taking in the situation, then, in stern tones, he demanded, "What
does this mean?"

Abbie glanced hurriedly at her husband. He
was a picture of cowardly fear. Every vestige of
color had left his face, and his hands hung listlessly
by his sides, while he stared at Abbie with a helpless, despairing look. As he caught her eye, he
tried to hold it with his own, but she turned resolutely away.

Mr. Saunders waited some moments for a reply,
then, seating himself near Abbie, he gently asked
her to tell her story. Thus admonished, she began
to recite what we already know.

She had not proceeded far before she was interrupted by her husband pronouncing the single
word, "Abbie!" Never, to her dying day, will she
forget the sound of that voice. Anger, fear,
entreaty, and despair were strangely blended in one
She glanced hurriedly at him, then continued her
narrative to the end.

Once more she heard his voice saying, "Abbie,
beware!" but she did not heed him, and continued
her story, never faltering, until she had told the

whole story. Then she cried, with touching earnestness, "And you will save me, will you not, O my father?"

Mr. Saunders turned to Mr. Deering (who had sat during the recital carelessly tipped back in his chair, his legs crossed, his pipe in his mouth, seemingly intent on watching the clouds of smoke as they curled upward to the ceiling, but listening carefully to every word), saying: "You hear, Mr. Deering? You will help me take her?"

Deering straightened back farther in his chair, and, thrusting his hands into his breeches pockets, slowly said, as he watched Steve intently: "She don't need no help. She can go where she pleases. The law will protect her."

A sigh of relief escaped Abbie's lips, then a sudden fear that that same law which would protect her in her freedom might snatch from her arms her darling child, took possession of her.

"But the babe?" she asked eagerly. "Can he take it from me?"

"No, he cannot take it under one year, in this State, I believe. In some it is two years, but not less than one in any State. And you may be able to get the sole control of her. In a case like this, where the father has proved himself unfit to care for it, I think you will have no trouble in gaining it."

Rushford sat quietly listening to what was said. He felt the coils drawing closer around him. Every particle of hope departed, and left him a veritable coward. He did not attempt to deny one word of her story. He knew that half had not been told. The mention of the law did not tend to make him less uneasy.

He did not speak until Mr. Saunders excitedly asked the rest to leave the room, as he wished to speak to Mr. Deering alone. All rose to obey, when Rushford, with a withering look at Mr. Saunders, said:—

"I think *you* had better go out than turn a sick woman and her babe out in the snow."

Mr. Saunders saw his blunder, and quickly stepped outside, followed by Deering. Abbie cast a scornful look at Rushford. So he had at last come to the conclusion that she was a sick woman, and entitled to some consideration. Why had he not thought of that before?

As the door closed, he came eagerly forward, and began to plead with her to forgive and befriend him now. The tables had been completely turned. He felt that this was his only chance, and he pleaded eloquently for forgiveness.

He had not long to plead, however, for the door soon opened, and Deering came in. Drawing Rushford to one side, he spoke a few words to him, then, turning to Abbie, he explained that her father had gone to order a conveyance for her, while he would proceed immediately to the village and procure the arrest of Rushford, who stood by, pale with excitement, not knowing what to do.

Seeing his indecision, Deering advised him to "cut stick and clear out" as soon as possible.

"But they can't arrest me," he said; "I have done nothing to condemn me."

Deering looked at him with that strange, amused smile for a moment or two, as if trying to determine if he was in earnest, then said: "Nothing? You have done nothing? Don't you know that story Mrs. Rushford told this morning, and which she has a witness to in that girl Roxy, if told in court would jug you tighter than whisky ever was jugged?"

"I don't quite understand how it can," said he incredulously. The whole thing had been a mere farce to him, a mere play. He did not remember what he had done, only that he had broken no bones, had taken no lives.

"Don't see how it can?" asked Deering, laughing heartily. "Well, you are the dullest one I've seen lately. I thought your wife was innocent enough, but you cap the climax," and he laughed again.

An angry flush overspread Rushford's face, and he said sulkily: "I can't see what you mean. What is there to laugh at? Can't you explain yourself?"

"Oh, yes, I can explain myself easy enough, I guess, so that even you can understand me!"

Striking an attitude, opening one hand and laying the forefinger of the other on it, and looking at

him in an aggravating way, that tempted Rushford
to strike him, he continued:—

"Now, don't you remember about your threatening your wife with death, about your taking down
that file, which would be termed an instrument of
death in such a case, of your throwing it into the
logs near your wife's head (I know you did that,
for I can count more than twenty marks in the
logs), to say nothing of your stuffing paper into
the baby's mouth? It might have choked her to
death, if it was the Bible. Now, if she tells that
story in court, and Roxy swears to it, I wouldn't
give much for your freedom for a while. Besides,
you'll sleep in jail to-night, any way, if you don't
clear out, and that mighty quick. Saunders is
mad, and he won't rest until you are got rid of."

The look of anger in Rushford's face gradually
changed to one of alarm as Deering proceeded,
and when he ceased speaking, it presented that
cowardly look of abject terror which it had worn
once before that day. He seemed to be undecided
how to act, and Deering once more urged him to
fly at once.

At last he seemed to make a decision, and, hastily gathering some of his clothes together, he
thrust them into a valise and left the room; then,
returning, he clasped Abbie's hands and bade her
good-by. As she shook his hand, she slipped
into it a few dollars—all she had. He looked up
with a grateful smile and left the room.

Abbie watched him out of sight, then the tears fell thick and fast. There was a strange tumult in her heart. When she thought of her own condition, a feeling of thankfulness prevailed. She felt that she could not live with him longer, but farther than this she had not calculated. She had no feelings of revenge against him, and would not have made an effort to punish him. To know that he was going out into the world, a fugitive from justice, seemed so terrible that she could but pity him. The sleigh soon arrived, and she was taken home. Home! how sweet the word sounded to her! Mrs. Saunders met her at the door with tears and a hearty welcome. Her little brothers and sisters crowded around her, welcoming her with warm kisses, then clamored to see the baby.

With pride the mother exhibited her darling, and received their simple words of admiration. But as she gazed upon her darling's face, a dreadful fear tugged at her heart. She might be forced to give her up at the end of a year. One short year! How very short it seemed! Could she have known that one short month would not pass ere her child would be ruthlessly torn from her grasp, how sweet one year's respite would have seemed!

Mr. Saunders soon returned with a weary look, saying that Steve had disappeared, and he had requested the sheriff not to pursue him.

"I thought as I was returning home," said he,

"of the process that must be gone through with if he was arrested, of the publicity into which it would bring our family, and I must say I was glad he was gone. Deering thinks he has scared him until he will not dare to show his face here again. If he will only stay away, it is all I ask."

Abbie felt much relieved. She too had dreaded the publicity of a trial in court, and she was well pleased with her father's decision.

The young men soon returned from their work and were surprised and pleased to see Abbie at home once more.

Raz caught up the baby, kissed it, and wondered how it would seem to be called uncle; then, noticing Abbie's sad face, asked her what was the matter. Before this question could be answered, Will asked: "Where have you left Steve? I don't see him."

There was a moment's pause. All eyes were turned toward Abbie, who trembled violently, while great tears fell from her eyes. Will's manner of badinage changed to one of alarm, and he turned to his mother for an explanation.

"I hope you will never see him here again," she said. "He has forfeited all claims to respect, and your sister does not wish to see him again."

"How? Why? What has he been doing?" asked both boys in a breath.

She explained in as few words as possible what she knew of the circumstances, adding:—

"I myself do not thoroughly understand it. Abbie will, no doubt, tell us all about it this evening, but as supper is ready now, let us say no more about it at present."

When they were gathered around the fire in the evening, Abbie told her story. Great was the excitement of all as she finished. The brothers declared that he should not escape. They would follow him to the ends of the earth but he should be punished. Then Mr. Saunders explained what he had done, to which they were much opposed.

"What!" they cried with one accord, "shall he treat our sister in this manner, and then be allowed to go away unmolested?—No, this is too much. He must be punished."

"But you forget! In order to punish him we must become the town talk, and your sister must be dragged before a courtroom, full of staring people, and swear to and repeat this story, which it pains her so much to tell to us. So you see by attempting to punish him, you must give her more pain, of which I judge she has had enough. No, my sons, if he has gone, as I hope and trust he has, let him go."

Abbie joined her pleadings with his, and they at last reluctantly consented.

"But are you sure he has gone?" asked Raz. "May he not be hiding somewhere near by?"

"No," said Mr. Saunders, "the officer followed him some distance. He has taken to the woods, and will, no doubt, be many miles away before morning."

"He may have done this to throw you off your guard. I do not believe he will leave us alone. He is too cruel and revengeful. We shall have trouble with him yet."

"I hope not. Mr. Deering thinks he will trouble us no more. He went with me to the house, and was a great help to me. If it had not been for him, I should have had trouble to get Abbie away. He understood the law better than I, and Steve saw there was no use to say anything. He stayed with her and saw Steve start but could not prevent him. He says he was about as scared a fellow as he ever saw, and will get as far away as possible before he stops."

"Well, maybe it's all right, but he isn't to be trusted. It won't be well for him to show himself around here, though," added Raz, as he strode away to his room.

Soon all retired, and midnight stillness reigned around.

Here we must take leave of them, and follow the footsteps of Steven Rushford.

.

8

CHAPTER X.

IT was with a strange commingling of emotion that he left the house and commenced his journey. A few moments before he had not thought of such a thing; but his conduct for the last few days, when held up before his mind's eye by Mr. Deering, took on a form of reality which startled him. What had before looked to him like a mere farce would, when told to others, take the form of real crime, and he saw the necessity of eluding the consequences if possible.

He saw that there was no way to do this but by immediate flight. So great had been his haste he had nearly forgotten to speak to Abbie. He could not realize his position. It seemed rather to be some fitful dream than reality. Then, as he thought of the charge that would be brought against him, and what the consequences might be, his heart quaked with fear, and he fled in wild haste down the road and into the woods.

Remembering the caution Deering had given him, he avoided the traveled road, taking the most unfrequented bypaths, and pressing forward with

(114)

all his might.   On, on he went, scarcely pausing to
take breath.

Late in the afternoon he found himself in a deep
ravine, completely sheltered from view, but so near
the road that, though no one could see him, he
could see and hear all who passed.   Here he sat
down to rest his weary limbs and think what course
to pursue.   Heretofore he had thought of nothing
but to put as great a distance as possible between
himself and danger.

But he had eaten nothing that day, and the
gnawings of hunger nearly unmanned him.   The
cold, too, was intense.   He could not remain out
all night.   What should he do?   As he realized
his desolate condition, his thoughts flew back to
Abbie.

He thought of his own cruel behavior; of her
patient endurance; how he had tried to drive her
to an attempt to leave him, that he might have
more with which to taunt her; how he had at last
been driven to that dreadful farce by which he
meant to clinch his power over her forever, but the
results of which had been so disastrous to himself;
of his flight from the house where he had been
wont to rule; of that last look of his injured wife,
in which was blended such a world of pity; of the
money she had placed in his hands, which she had
earned by her needle while unable to get out, and
was hoarding so carefully.

She had thought of his comfort before her own

even then. Now that he seemed parted from her forever, he remembered her good qualities with regret. Yet, mingled with this feeling, was one of regret that she had escaped his power. The thought that she was safe and happy with her friends, warmed and fed, while he sat shivering here like a culprit, with neither food nor fire, was more than his nature could bear.

A terrible thirst for revenge came over him. He clinched his fists and ground his teeth, while a look of malignity distorted his features. He strode out boldly into the highway, and began to retrace his steps. The sun was just sinking in the west, and the dark shadows began to creep into the recesses of the woods, growing deeper and deeper, but he did not heed them.

All fear of detection seemed to have left him. Soon a bright light gleamed out before him. It came from the window of a small cabin near the road. He recognized the place, and, walking boldly up to the door, he knocked and was admitted. The cabin was occupied by a widow and her two daughters. They greeted him cordially. He told them he had been belated, and, as he was very hungry and had a good distance to walk, he would like a bite to eat.

The kind-hearted woman set before him a substantial meal, of which he ate heartily, and then resumed his journey, where we will leave him for a while, as we visit with our reader the home of Mr. Deering.

It is a small frame house, situated about one-quarter of a mile from Mr. Saunders' residence, and within plain view from their door.

On approaching it, near the hour of ten, we perceive a light still streaming from a window in the sitting room. We enter, and find the room deserted by all except Mr. Deering, who sits tipped back in his chair—a position he invariably assumes upon sitting down—his hands crossed idly on his breast, his face having an absorbed expression, as he gazes through the grate at the glowing coals, and puffs fitfully at the pipe which he holds between his lips. Occasionally he smiles slightly—that strange, odd smile he is wont to wear when amused. He was, no doubt, thinking of the events of the morning, which to him had been highly amusing.

His early life had been spent in roving over the country. He led for some years the life of a scout, and had seen some lively times, as he expressed it, and this quiet, humdrum life was getting tedious. The events of the morning promised to break its monotony, and so could not fail to give him some pleasure.

"Of course," he said to himself, "they will come together again, and kiss, and make up, and all that sort of thing, but I like to see a little fun out of it first. This life is so unbearably dull! I've almost a mind to do something terrible myself, just to raise a breeze, though I don't exactly approve of

playing with women and babies as that fellow
Rushford has been doing. What a brute the man
must be! She'll be a fool if she does go back.
And Saunders," he continued, "I was surprised to
hear him say he should not have him followed.
If that was my girl, now, I'd follow him to the ends
of the earth before he should escape. I wonder
where the coward is now? Far enough away from
here, I reckon, and won't want to come back in a
hurry, either. Didn't I scare him though?" and
he laughed aloud. He'll not show his face here
again."

But in this he was mistaken, for scarcely had the
last words left his lips when he heard a quick,
energetic knock on the door. Rising hastily, he
opened it and peered out into the darkness. To
his surprise, he was confronted by the tall, burly
form of Rushford, who did not stop to be invited
in, but stalked boldly into the room.

"To what am I indebted for this visit?" asked
Deering, as soon as he could recover from his surprise sufficiently to speak. "I supposed you were
far enough away from here by this time, and more
likely to go farther than to return."

"In that you were mistaken," replied Rushford,
trying to assume a look of bravery which he was
far from feeling, as he gazed questioningly into the
face of Mr. Deering.

"So I see," said Deering, seeming scarcely to
know whether to be pleased or not with his visitor.

"But again I ask, to what am I indebted for this visit?"

"I scarcely know what answer to make," said Rushford, his face assuming a half-defiant, half-troubled look. "You were at the house this morning, and heard the reasons my wife gave for going away, and it was by your advice that I left. You was my friend then; now I want to know if you will be my friend still."

He looked straight into the eyes of Deering, who looked very much annoyed. To be sure, he had helped him away, but his sympathies had been with the wife, and he did not relish being called a friend by one who had taken the course Rushford had. He motioned Rushford to a chair, and, taking one himself, said:—

"I don't know as what I did for you gives you a right to call me a friend. I'm sure I don't approve of your conduct at all."

"But you helped me away," persisted Rushford. "I should not have gone a step if it had not been for you."

"Well, yes, I advised you to go, because, you see, I couldn't stand by and see a man nabbed, and say nothing. But if it had been my girl you had treated so, I'll be bound you wouldn't escape."

"I was a brute with her, I know," said Rushford penitently, for he saw that that character would be the best he could assume.

He had started back with the determination to

be avenged on old Saunders, as he called him, but as he drew nearer the spot, his courage failed him. He thought if he could get someone to stand by him, he would be all right. But who could he get? He thought of Deering and came to the conclusion to try him. He was glad to find him up, and at once determined to make a friend of him if possible.

"But I am sorry, and want to make up with her," he continued.

"But do you think she will make up with you?" asked Deering.

"I hope so. I think if I can get a chance to talk with her, I can make it all right. Why," he added, enthusiastically, "she is one of the quietest little women in the world. She would do anything rather than oppose me."

"Then I should have thought you would have prized her more."

"So I ought, and if you will help me get her back, I promise to treat her well."

An angry flush overspread the face of Deering, and he said: "Now look here, Rushford, if you think I am going to get the whole neighborhood down on me by helping you do your brutish work, you are mistaken. I ain't your man. If you mean what you say about treating the girl well, and she will listen to you, all right. But I shan't have anything to do with it."

"Of course I don't expect you to have anything

to do with it," said Rushford. "All I want is a chance to hide, and a place to hide, until I get a chance to see her alone. Then, if she won't listen, it's all right. Just let me stay here, and I promise it will be all right."

"But Saunders will be after you if he sees you here," objected Deering.

"I suppose he's after me now, only I guess he's off the track," said Rushford laughing.

"No, he ain't. When he found you had cut sticks and run for it, he told the officer to let you go, if you would only stay away. I told him you would do that fast enough, so he has gone home contented, believing you to be far away."

Rushford was silent and thoughtful for some time. He was much surprised at the leniency of Mr. Saunders, and relieved to find that he was not pursued. He grew self-possessed and calm, and determined to push through this trouble and secure Abbie again.

Turning once more to Deering, he said, "At least, you will let me stay here to-night?"

Deering did not refuse, but showed him to a room, and then retired himself.

Thus it happened that while Abbie and her friends slept securely, believing their enemy miles away, he was safely housed only a quarter of a mile away, where he could watch their every motion, and ascertain when they should leave Abbie alone. He determined to watch his chance when the men were all away, then go boldly in, and, if Abbie would not go with him, make his threat good by taking the child. She should never bring his child up in that house.

While making his plans for future operation, he fell asleep, and, owing to his fatigue, did not wake until the short winter day was far advanced. When he entered the family room, he met Mrs. Deering, a quiet, sweet-tempered woman, in the midst of her household duties. She had prepared his breakfast, which was waiting for him, and of which he partook heartily. Then, as Mr. Deering did not appear, he inquired where he had gone, and was told that he had gone to the village.

He sat down at a window which overlooked the grounds of Mr. Saunders. No one seemed to be stirring, and he carelessly asked if they had left the house. Mrs. Deering did not reply, but little Danny, a boy of ten years, said he saw them go by to the woods, just at daylight. His mother gave him a reproving look, but the mischief was done. Rushford rose hastily and left the house.

Passing around to the back of the house, so that he should not be discovered and thus give Abbie a chance to escape, he crept silently up, until he gained a side of Mr. Saunders' house where there were no windows. Here he paused and listened. Not a sound was to be heard, and, gaining courage, he passed boldly around and entered the front door. No one was in the room but Mrs. Saunders and Roxy.

He bowed with mock politeness to Mrs. Saunders, who rose and quietly asked him to leave the
house. His only reply was to ask to see Abbie.

"She is in the kitchen," said Mrs. Saunders, "but
she does not wish to see you," at the same time
stepping before the door to intercept his movements.

Thrusting her rudely aside, he flung open the
door. Abbie was seated by the stove with her
baby in her arms. At sight of them he stepped
forward, but was confronted by Raz, who bade him
leave the house. As he showed no inclination to
obey, Raz presented a pistol and again ordered
him to leave. He turned to retrace his steps, pushing Mrs. Saunders rudely against the wall as he
did so, then fled precipitately, as Raz, angered at
the treatment his mother received, emptied one
barrel of the pistol at his head.

The bullet flew wide of its mark, and no harm
was done to the fugitive, who, as soon as he was
well out of danger, stopped his mad flight to consider what was to be done next. He was now convinced that they would be on the watch, and unless
he could get rid of Raz, he would not be allowed
to speak to Abbie. He studied some time, and at
last hit upon a plan. He could have Raz arrested
for firing on him, and then, as soon as he was gone,
he could get into the house with no one to molest
him. While he is gone for this purpose, we will go
back and learn how Raz happened to be near at
the right time.

It had been decided at the breakfast table that it would not be prudent to leave the house alone, and Raz was appointed to stay. He was in the barn at work and happened to go to the door just in time to see Rushford leave Mr. Deering's house. He recognized him at once, and, thinking his movements rather suspicious, had watched him until aware of his plan; then he slipped, unobserved by him, into the house, and informed his mother and sisters of what was going on.

They stationed themselves as Rushford found them, and were hardly settled before he entered. Raz would have stationed himself at the outer door had not Mrs. Saunders, fearing bloodshed, and believing that Rushford would obey her, insisted upon this plan. But she found that the man who could be cruel to his wife and laugh at her pain, would not scruple to lay rude hands upon her if she stood in his way. She realized more than ever how cruel must have been the position of her child in the power of such a man.

As for Raz, he could hardly be restrained from following and shooting him like a dog. They were still talking over the affair when a rap was heard at the door. On opening it they met the good-natured face of the village constable, who shook Raz by the hand and asked what this all meant, adding that he had a warrant for his arrest. Raz at once told him, in as few words as possible, what had happened.

"Then, if I arrest you, the ladies will be left unprotected?" asked the officer.

"That is exactly how it stands, and I think that is
his game. He treated my sister with the greatest
cruelty, even threatening her life, and then pretended to leave the country, but came back after
dark, and was harbored by Deering. He hid there
until he thought we were all off for the day, and
then came here. No knowing what might have
happened if I had not been here."

"He is an ugly-looking chap," said the officer,
looking toward Rushford, who stood a short distance away, looking on with an exultant smile,
"and I believe he means mischief."

"I am sure he does," said Raz. "That is just
his game, you will see."

The officer stood silent for some time, then said
thoughtfully: "I don't know what to do. I don't
like the look of things at all. But you know I
have no right to judge of a case. If I do my duty,
the ladies will be left at his mercy, and I would not
trust him a minute. I have a mind to tear up my
warrant and run the risk of losing my position."

"No need of that," said Raz, who had been watching the approach of a horseman who was coming
toward them at a rapid rate. "My brother is coming, and I will go with you."

The officer glanced at the newcomer; then, laying his hand on the shoulder of Raz, said in a loud
tone, intended to reach the ear of Rushford, who

still stood at a distance, "Erastus Saunders, I arrest you in the name of the law."

A wicked smile crossed the face of Rushford as he heard these words; then, catching the sound of horse's hoofs, he turned and saw the approach of Anda. The smile changed to a look of anger, and he walked hurriedly away.

The situation was explained to Anda, and Raz was preparing to accompany the officer, when he inquired: "But how did you happen to come so opportunely? We were in a great quandary and did not know what to do."

"I did," interrupted the officer. "I would have thrown up my commission before I would have taken Raz away."

"Good for you! Let's shake hands on that!" exclaimed Anda, seizing his hand with a hearty grip.

Raz was much affected by the behavior of the officer. They had been merely speaking acquaintances before, but from that time they were firm friends.

Anda then told his story, which was simple enough. He had been to the village and met Mr. Deering, who told him that Rushford was back in the neighborhood, and he had ridden over to see if all was right.

"You came in the nick of time," said Raz. "Now I'll forgive that Deering. I was so mad when I found he had harbored Rushford I could have killed him."

"If it had not been for him, I should not have been here," said Anda. "So save your anger for some better cause."

"You will have cause enough, if I am not mistaken," said Rush, the officer. "That man has got the devil in him, and he will give you trouble enough unless you can get rid of him."

"I am sure of it," said Raz, "and I don't like to be away overnight. It leaves father, who is old, and Will all alone. I suppose there will have to be a trial before I can get away?"

"Yes, but that can easily be fixed," said Rush. "We can have the trial come off this afternoon and get home to-night."

"Good!" said Raz, much relieved. "That will 'be capital, so let us be off at once. You must keep a sharp lookout," he added to Anda as he rode away.

"And have the witnesses there at four," called Rush.

Anda entered the house and greeted his mother and sister. He answered their many questions, then asked one himself: "What has been the trouble, dear sister? I am anxious to know, for I have heard nothing but what Deering told me this morning, and I should like to hear the story from your own lips."

While Abbie answers his question, we will answer one which has no doubt entered the mind of our reader: Where had Anda been? and why did he not know of his sister's trouble?

We answer: Anda had married about three months before his sister, and was now living some distance from them, near his wife's parents. This was but the second day since her parents had heard of her trouble, so he had heard nothing about it.

Anda was Abbie's favorite brother, because of his kind, gentle ways, and his tender thoughtfulness of her comfort. He had taken the position of young manhood just as Abbie began to throw off the tastes and habits of little girlhood, so it happened that it was he who had taken her to the picnics, and shared her pleasant drives or horseback rides through the country. They had grown to love one another more than is usually the case with brother and sister.

As she now poured the tale of her trouble into his eager ear, she felt sure of his tender sympathy. Oh, how sweet were these assurances to her hungry heart!

CHAPTER XI.

MR. SAUNDERS returned before they started for the village, and accompanied them to the court room. Raz was acquitted in due form, and the crowd broke up amid great excitement.

Just as Mr. Saunders was about to drive away, the justice came eagerly, elbowing his way through the crowd, and called out in a loud voice, "Here, you young chap," motioning to Raz, "come this way a minute. I want to speak to you."

He led the way into his private room, Raz following him and dreading a reprimand. What was his surprise to see him take from the rack where it had been resting a small six-barreled revolver, and, after wiping the dust from it, examine it carefully. At last he seemed satisfied, and turned to his astonished visitor.

"Do you call that shooting iron of yours the best to be had?"

"By no means," said Raz. "To tell the truth, I was ashamed to show it. It is an old one that my brother got in some trade. We have never paid

9   (129)

any attention to it, as we don't have much use for anything of that kind at our house."

"If I mistake not," said the justice, "you will have need enough for one now. If I am a judge of human nature, that rascal will give you plenty of trouble yet. I don't like the look of him a bit and I can't see for the life of me how that quiet, sensible-looking sister of yours came to have anything to do with him."

"His mother and mine were old friends, and he lived with us a long time. I never liked him much, but would not have believed him such a rascal."

"Well, I was going to say if you like you can take this shooting iron, and use it as long as you please. If you can't settle him with that, I am sorry for you. Protect the ladies and the law will protect you."

Raz was surprised and thankful for this token of friendship, and thanked him heartily. He not only had a better weapon, but he had made a friend for which he felt more grateful than he could have thought possible a few days before.

He hurried out, thinking he had kept them all waiting, but found that they had hardly noticed his absence. They were surrounded by a group of friends, who had left their warm firesides to assure them of their sympathy. It has been said that "a friend in need is a friend indeed." Never had friendship seemed so precious to them as now, when they so much needed it.

"You had better take my advice," said one white-haired old gentleman, as they drove away.

The drive home was a silent one. Each was busy with his own thoughts. They found a warm supper ready for them on their arrival, to which they did ample justice.

Soon they were seated around the cheerful fire, which, after their cold ride, seemed unusually pleasant. But, though it gave forth its brightest glow, none seemed to heed, and none but sad faces were turned toward it.

At last Mr. Saunders said: "I scarcely know what to do about it. Mr. Corbit says we will not be free of that fellow unless we adopt severe measures, and many others seem to share his opinion. There seems to be no other course to pursue but to have him arrested."

Mrs. Saunders looked up suddenly: "I did hope that could be avoided."

"So did I. It is very disagreeable indeed, but you know it would not be safe to leave the house at all. Neither you nor Abbie would be safe an hour if we were to leave you alone, and we need to be chopping every day."

"But what can we do?" asked Raz.

"Corbit says he should advise me to have him arrested."

"That's just what Rush and the officer say," said Raz. "All are agreed in saying that we have a hard customer to deal with, and that we have got to stop fooling or we'll go under."

"Yes, all are agreed on that," said Will, "and I should not wonder if he was up to some deviltry now."

"I guess not. He's too big a coward to come out in the night."

"Don't you fool yourself, Raz. You'll find he has got pluck enough when he can be doing something mean. By the way, where is that old shooting iron of mine?"

"It is in its place, you'll find if you look."

Will took it down with a comical air of concern, and looked it all over carefully.

"I say, Raz, how did you do it? It don't strike fire half the time for me."

"It did this time," said Raz, as he remembered the scene, which looked quite amusing now; "and somebody got outside the door quicker than he ever did the trick before, I guess."

"I suppose he thought it *might* make a mistake and go off. He made fun enough of it when I got it."

"It was not pointed at his head then. That makes all the difference in the world with a man's feelings," laughed Raz. "At least, I think it would with mine."

"No doubt. But I don't like the idea that this is all we have got in the shape of a weapon. It might not behave so well next time."

Mr. Saunders sat quietly watching the embers, not appearing to take any notice of the conversation, but he looked up now.

"What did the justice want of you, Raz?"

"Just a little advice and assistance, sir."

"I suppose he advised you to steer clear of shooting irons, didn't he?" asked Will.

"On the contrary, he presented me with a better one, and advised me to use it with more accuracy next time."

"Presented you with a better one!" cried Will in astonishment. "And pray where is it?"

"Here," said Raz, drawing it from under his coat, where it had been unnoticed, and holding it toward Will.

Will took it with a burst of admiration. "Whew, isn't she a beauty though!" and he turned it over and over, gazing fondly at it. "Wouldn't I like to own it!"

Was there ever a boy who did not admire a nice new shooting iron. Will had been secretly proud of his, but this put it all in the shade. It was indeed a masterpiece, and both boys were proud of the possession of the beautiful weapon.

"But how did he happen to give it to you?" asked Will. "Did you borrow it?"

"No, he offered it himself. I noticed that he examined the old one some in the court room, and just as I was going to get into the sleigh, he called me back and into his room. I expected he wanted to caution me about using firearms, and was ready to use my tongue in my own defense, when, to my surprise, he gave me this revolver, saying it was his opinion we would need it."

Mr. Saunders had not spoken again. The sight of the revolver produced a different effect upon him than it did upon his sons. It brought sad forebodings of the future, and he at once resolved to have Steve arrested before more trouble overtook them. He advised Raz to be careful how he used the plaything in his hands, else he might get into trouble.

Raz told him what the justice had said, then described the scene of the morning more plainly, saying he should be sorry to use it, but no man should lay hands on his mother as he had seen done that morning, with impunity.

"I hope you do not think I am wrong, do you, father?" he added.

"No, my son. We must protect your mother and sister at all hazards, but I dread bloodshed, and think I shall have him arrested. It may save one or more lives."

They continued the conversation some time and concluded to get out another warrant in the morning. All due precautions were taken to secure their safety, and then all retired.

Abbie went to bed, but not to sleep. Her thoughts were too busy with painful memories, and too much troubled with anxiety for the future. The conversation of her brothers had been very painful to her, yet she could say nothing against the course proposed, or against the preparations for defense.

She knew the relentless disposition of their common enemy better than they. She had felt his

power, and knew that he would hesitate at nothing
that would wreak his vengeance upon any who had
offended him. Any attempt at reconciliation would
only make matters worse. He professed great love
for his wife and child, now that they were out of
his reach, but she knew that it was only for effect;
neither the cries of the child nor the tears and
entreaties of his wife could move him from any
cruel purpose, if once they were in his power.

She believed that if he set his will upon obtaining
them again, he would hesitate at nothing to gain
his ends, and her heart was filled with painful forebodings as she saw the preparations for self-defense
made by her brothers, for she believed their hands
would soon be stained with blood unless something
intervened to prevent it.

Even as they talked, her heart went up to the
throne of grace in prayer that they might be prevented from shedding blood. The answer came
quickly back, "Trust in God, my child." When
Mr. Saunders made known his intentions, she
thanked God for even this slight hope of relief,
though she did not forget that this step, if success-
fully accomplished, would bring its own trials.

It was a terrible thought to the young and gentle
Abbie to stand up before a court of justice and testify against the one she had sworn to love, honor,
and obey. The longer she thought of this, the
harder it seemed. She even thought of giving up
the struggle, and going back, but she thought of

her babe, and felt that this was the greater evil. There was nothing for her to do but "trust in God," and wait. With these reflections she fell asleep.

She was hardly dressed in the morning when she was informed that Steve was out at the well and wished to speak to her. She was greatly troubled, and did not know how to act. Her father had gone to the village, but her mother, seeing her indecision, advised her to go and see what he wanted. Perhaps he really wished to speak to her, and would go away after the interview. She decided to see him, at least for a moment.

Great as was her anxiety, she could not suppress a smile—first of amusement, then of contempt—as her eyes rested upon the figure before her. His hat was crushed in at the top, and his hair, which was rather long, was filled with straw and chaff. He was muffled up to the chin, and muffler, coat, and all were ornamented in the same manner as his hair. His face wore a woe-begone look, and, as she approached him, he came forward with a tottering step. Grasping her hand, he began a very touching speech which he had prepared for the occasion.

Abbie knew, as soon as she saw him, that he was trying another farce, but the whole thing was so clumsily prepared and so greatly overdrawn that she could not prevent a hearty laugh, which was echoed by her brothers, who had witnessed the whole performance.

As he heard the laughter, his expression changed to one of shame and confusion. He was perfectly nonplussed, and if he had had any important reason for requesting an interview, he forgot it, and, after talking a few minutes, in a confused sort of way took his leave, and Abbie entered the house.

Mrs. Saunders noticed the amused look on her face and asked what had happened, adding, "I thought the interview would be very unpleasant to you, and was surprised to hear you laugh, as though very much amused."

Abbie laughed again, then said: "I would not have believed when I opened the door this morning that anything could make me laugh. But, mother, if you had gone out with me, I am sure you would have laughed too."

Mrs. Saunders, greatly puzzled, asked: "What did you see to laugh at? I don't understand it at all."

Abbie told her what had occurred, at which she looked more puzzled than ever.

"What object could he have in doing such a thing?"

"Why, don't you see, mother? He wanted to make me believe that his condition is deplorable without a wife; that he is a homeless wanderer, and thus touch my sympathies; but the farce was too ridiculous. I have seen many a farce since I married him, but none quite so ridiculous as this, before. Just as though, when I saw him enter Mr.

Deering's house last night, I could believe him to be in such a forlorn condition to-day. But it is no new thing for him to try to deceive me, and I suppose, because I held my tongue and let it pass, he thinks I was deceived, and can be made to believe anything."

Will and Raz just then entered. Will was saying: "He walked like a knee-sprung horse. I wonder where he learned that gait. I say, Abbie, what do you suppose that fellow got himself up like that for? It beat everything I have ever seen."

"For ridiculousness, yes," said Abbie, in an annoyed tone. Now that she had had her laugh, the absurdity of the scene vexed her.

Raz seemed to share this feeling, and, taking a seat beside her, asked her opinion of the performance.

"Did he think we were all fools?" he asked.

"He seemed to think I am one," Abbie replied bitterly. "It is not the first time he has tried to deceive me in that manner. When I lived with him, I said nothing and let it pass, always acting, as far as possible, as though I believed him, and I suppose he thought I was such a fool that I did not know any better. O brother, I never have—I never can tell you one-half I have suffered with that man. He began to deceive me before we had been married twenty-four hours, and he has continued to torture and deceive me ever since. I begin to believe that he has always deceived me."

"How did he deceive you so soon?" asked Raz.
"I don't understand you."

"You remember the evening after we were married, when we were in the kitchen with the door locked?"

Raz did not remember, but Will said: "Yes, indeed, I remember! I thought you would eat up all the pies."

"Not much pie did we eat."

Then she related what happened then, which the reader already knows.

All waited with breathless interest until she had completed her story.

"O mother," she cried, when her story was finished, "you never could guess what I suffered that night, and many succeeding ones! I fully believed him to be insane, and suffered as much as though that had really been the case."

"But why did you not tell us, my child. It was very dangerous to keep such a thing still. Think what your fate might have been."

"I did think, dear mother. I did think—think—think, until I was nearly wild, yet something seemed to seal my lips and prevent me from speaking. I now think it was all for the best. What good would it have done to tell it? No one would have believed me, for, you may depend upon it, he would never have had another crazy spell, and I should not only have made him angry, but would have gained the name of prattler, and so received no sympathy when real trouble came. No, I think it was best for me to keep still. But if it had not been for your last words before my marriage, dear mother, I never could have borne it," she added softly.

"What were they?" asked Raz.

"They were, 'Trust in God, my child.' Those precious words have come to my mind in every trial, and I have found them no false reed to lean upon. Though they have not taken away the trouble, they have given me strength to bear it."

"They are indeed precious words," said Raz, in subdued tones.

"And we will trust in him, my brother."

"Not by sitting still and holding our hands, though. Do you think we do wrong to protect ourselves, Abbie?"

"No, indeed! 'God helps those who help themselves.' But you must not let your feelings run away with you."

"It is rather hard to govern them under such provocation, but I think your advice is good, and I will try to follow it."

"If you will all take Abbie's motto for a guide," said Mrs. Saunders, "you will be safe."

CHAPTER XII.

MR. SAUNDERS returned about noon with the intelligence that Steve had been arrested, and they would be safe from further annoyance in that direction. Then, turning to Abbie, he said:—

"It is thought best that you should apply for a divorce at once, so that all can be settled."

"But is it necessary for me to do so, father?"

"It is, my daughter, if you do not intend to return to him."

"Oh, no, never!" cried Abbie quickly. "I have no intention of doing such a thing. Indeed, I could not."

"Very well, then, it is necessary for you to have a divorce as soon as possible, both for your own sake and your child," said her father gravely. "While you remain as you are, he will molest you continually; but if you have a divorce, he will be apt to give up. Besides, you can make no move towards getting permanent control of your child until you apply for a divorce. Lawyer Price thinks it had better be all done at once, and I have made

(141)

arrangements for you to be there to-morrow morning in time to arrange matters before the trial, which will be at ten o'clock. Of course you will have to be there for that."

"Very well, I will go," said Abbie, rising and leaving the room.

She wished to be alone, and, entering her own room, she flung herself upon her bed, and gave way to a passionate fit of weeping. As the difficulties and trials of her pathway loomed up before her, she felt entirely unfit for the struggle. There seemed to be no end to the long, dark hill of adversity she was doomed to climb, no resting-place for her weary feet. She must climb on, on if she hoped to gain rest at last.

Rest! Oh, how sweet the word sounded to her weary ears! Could it ever be? Was there a time even in the far-off future when she could rest, with nothing to molest or make her afraid, when she could enjoy the sweet comfort of home?

The picture was a bright one to contemplate, too bright, far too bright, she told herself with a feeling of despair, far too bright to be true. No, she must, however unwillingly, turn from this picture to the stern reality. She must look this fresh trouble in the face and prepare to meet it. But, oh, how weak and incapable she felt!

She knew that the enemy she had to deal with was relentless as fate, that she could hope for nothing from him but trouble, yet her heart shrank within her as she thought of appearing in a court of justice and testifying against the father of her child. Had he been a hundred times more guilty, she would have shrunk from the ordeal.

She thought of the grief and mortification his parents, brothers, and sisters would feel when they should hear of his trial, and her heart bled for them. Then she thought of her own position, past, present, and future, of her babe, whom she must guard at all hazards.

Falling upon her knees, she prayed God to guide her in all her trials, and help her to put her trust in him. A sweet feeling of trust stole over her, and she rose from her knees greatly strengthened and began her preparations for the morrow. She knew literally nothing of what would be required of her, and, therefore, could do nothing but wait and trust.

The morrow came and they set out for the village, where they arrived in safety. The court room was filled to overflowing. Abbie was called to the desk, where a petition for divorce which had been drawn up was read to her, to which she signed her name. She and Roxy were then led to the witness stand, and the trial began.

It is needless to describe the formula, which is understood by nearly everyone at the present day. It was a terrible ordeal for these two young women, neither of whom had ever seen the inside of a court room before, to sit up there in the witness box, the target for every eye.

When the stern voice of the judge was heard calling the assembly to order, and Abbie was called to be sworn, she tottered to her feet like one suddenly bereft of strength. She lifted her heart to God in prayer for strength, which gradually returned, and she became calm and firm. Her face was pale, but her eyes shone with an unwonted fire.

She met unflinchingly the eye of the judge, as he repeated, in slow and solemn tones, the oath by which she must be sworn. A deathlike stillness reigned throughout the room. When the time came for her to speak the words that bound her to speak the truth, the whole truth, and nothing but the truth, her voice was clear and calm; and when requested to tell her story, she did so in such a straightforward, frank manner that it carried conviction to every heart, and caused a look of dismay to settle over the countenances of the defendant and his counsel. They had hoped much from hesitation in her story.

Roxy was then sworn, and, though she was not so clear and explicit, her testimony corroborated that of Abbie.

The court proceeded in the usual manner. Speeches were made "pro and con." The council for the defendant used all his eloquence to destroy the evidence of the sisters. He branded the whole thing as a " put-up job," representing his client as a gentle, loving father and tender husband, whom this unnatural wife and her unprincipled father were trying to rob of his only child (at which said client used his handkerchief freely, though it remained perfectly dry). He begged the jury not to let themselves be deceived by two "chits of girls," and drawn on to do an act of unprecedented cruelty to a suffering brother, and ended with a great flourish by recommending his client to the favor and clemency of the jury.

There was a buzz of dissatisfaction throughout the room as he resumed his seat.

He was followed by Squire Price, counsel for the plaintiff, of which there were two of the best in the county engaged,—Squire Price and Captain Johns.

Squire Price commenced his plea by saying that he should spend no time in attempting to repute the speech of his opponent, as, in his opinion, it refuted itself; that his brother attorney reminded him of a remark he had heard made in reference to the devil —he had overshot the mark. In attempting to hedge his client in by all the graces of virtue and injured innocence, while he termed the injured wife and mother a "chit of a girl," and warned the jury not to be deceived by her, he had plainly shown the jury that he was working, not for justice, but to win his case.

He had, he said, great confidence in the judgment and integrity of the jury, and felt that they would consider well the testimony of the witnesses, and be guided thereby. The testimony was so plain that no one who heard it could doubt that the defendant,

10

so far from being a tender, loving husband, had been
a cruel, heartless tyrant, committing outrages upon
his defenseless wife that should not escape the punishment of the law, and crowning all by threatening
her life.   If this was showing his affection, he had
his opinion of it.

There was great applause throughout his speech,
and when he sat down the house resounded with
cheers.   The jury, after a few moments' absence,
returned a verdict of guilty, and Steve was remanded
to jail.   Mr. Saunders and his family returned home
with strong hopes that their worst trouble was over,
but scarcely twelve hours had passed before they
were notified that another trial would be given the
defendant, which they must attend in ten days from
that time.

Mr. Crosswell, attorney for defendant, had really
set himself to work, and seemed determined to
clear him.

This was sad news for Abbie.   She had hoped
for rest too soon.   She must still endure sorrow,
grief, and pain.

The final trial for her divorce and custody of her
child would not come off until court set, in March,
and it was only the beginning of December.

Her council had explained to her that, although
the father could not take the child forcibly from
her arms, yet, if he could get possession of it without
violence, the law could not touch him, and she was
in constant dread lest he should do this crowning
piece of wickedness.

She had seen by his looks and actions during the trial that he was in no way changed, that his thirst for revenge was not yet satisfied. To know that she suffered would only spur him on to greater deeds of violence. She also felt sure that he had a willing ally in the person of his counsel, who was an evil-minded man, whom none employed except when they could get no other to espouse their cause.

It relieved her uneasiness in a measure to know that her enemy was under lock and key. But she had yet to learn the uncertainty of human hopes. How truly it has been said, "Where ignorance is bliss 'tis folly to be wise."

CHAPTER XIII.

RUSHFORD ESCAPES AND APPEARS AS A GHOST.

IME passed and only one night intervened before the trial. There was no moon, and it would have been very dark but for the light snow that had fallen through the evening.

All in the house were wrapped in slumber, when, about two o'clock, Abbie was awakened by hearing her name called in a well-known voice, which made her blood curdle in her veins and her heart leap for fear. She held her breath and listened. Could she have been mistaken? Was it only a dream? She had almost persuaded herself that this was the case, when her name, called in the same terrible tones, again broke the midnight stillness that reigned around.

There was a sudden movement in her brothers' room, and Abbie knew that one or both of them were awake. Soon, as if the visitant were aware that he had hearers, the voice was heard again, hollow and unearthly.

It stated that it had been summoned by superhuman power, and sent to warn Abbie, and the inhabitants of that house, not to appear against one

(148)

Steven Rushford, who was wrongfully held in custody.   If they heeded not this warning, a sudden
and terrible punishment would come upon them.

Raz could stand this no longer.   Springing to the
window, he threw up the sash, and thrust out his
head, just in time to see a figure, draped in white,
disappear around the corner.   He stood in perfect
silence for a moment, trying to realize the situation.
Then, as it dawned upon him in all its ridiculous
absurdity, he burst forth in a hearty peal of laughter,
joined by Will, who had followed him, and had
also caught sight of the flying figure.

"Well, well, well! if that isn't about the coolest
thing I have heard of lately!" said Raz, as soon as
he could speak for laughing.   "I knew that man
was up to all sorts of deviltry, but I did not think
him capable of such a ridiculous performance as
this."

"What does he take us for?" said Will, with
another laugh.

"Just to think," continued Raz, "that he should
try to deceive us by such a flimsy affair as that.   I
suppose he expected we would think it was a spirit,
or an angel sent to warn us.   As if he could per-
sonate an angel, or a spirit either, for that matter,
though he must have the spirit of the devil in him
as big as a woodchuck, as Dutch George says."

" Yes," said Will, "and he no doubt thought that
we would be too frightened to recognize his voice.
He must believe himself good at acting."

"Abbie, are you awake?" called Raz.

"Yes," she answered.

"Did you hear that terrible warning?"

"Every word."

"What do you think of it?"

"I think I have heard the gentleman who delivered that warning say some silly things before."

"So you knew the voice?"

"Yes, indeed, perfectly well. But I thought he
was locked up. How do you suppose he got out?"

"Got out?" echoed Raz. "Why, that old rat
trap of a jail wouldn't hold a fool if they tried to
get out."

"Do you suppose he has gone?" asked Will.
"I haven't heard a sound since he turned the corner."

"I am going down to see," replied Raz, in a reso-
lute voice, as he opened his room door, "and if he
don't want more fun than he bargained for, he had
better make himself scarce pretty suddenly."

As the door closed behind him, there was a sudden sound of footsteps at the corner where the ap-
parition had disappeared. When he opened the
outer door, nothing was to be seen, though he distinctly heard the retreating footsteps. He listened
until they were no longer audible, and then re-
entered the house. To say that he was vexed at
this petty annoyance would hardly do him justice.
As he was passing his father's door, his voice was
heard asking the cause of the disturbance. Raz

briefly explained what had happened, and then passed on to his room.

"The rascal stood by and heard all we said," cried Will, as Raz entered the room. "I heard him leave the house as you went down."

"I suspected as much," replied Raz. "That was what sent me down."

"Seems to me spirits make more noise in walking than storybooks give them credit for," said Will.

"And show more discretion in regard to cold lead," added Raz. "But we must drop this interesting subject if we want to get any sleep to-night."

The others seemed to be of the same opinion, and all was quiet for the next two hours, when the family began to be astir, and preparations were made to start for the village.

Raz was especially impatient to be off. "I want plenty of time before court sets," he said, "and if Steven Rushford does not make up his mind, before twenty-four hours pass, that this is the worst night's work he ever did, I'll lose my guess."

Abbie started when she heard this threat. She knew her brother's impulsive disposition, and feared that he would commit some crime. But she need have had no fear, for Raz had no intention of committing any crime. He had a far better plan than that to make Steve ashamed of his night's work.

He saw the look of fear on her face, and returned it with a mischievous smile, which somewhat reassured her, though she watched him with more than common interest when they arrived at the village. She saw him call Squire Price to one side, where they held a short consultation. Her brother stood with his back toward her, but she could see the face of Squire Price distinctly.

At the first words of young Saunders a look of surprise overspread his face, followed, as he continued his story, by one of incredulity and amusement, and as he finished he burst into a hearty fit of laughter. Slapping Raz upon the back, he said good-humoredly:—

"Come, come, Saunders, all this trouble and worry must be turning your brain. A ghost, did you say? Who ever heard of such nonsense at this time of the world? No, no, you must be trying to fool me. You surely cannot believe in ghosts?"

All eyes were by this time directed toward the two men, for who does not become instantly interested at the mention of ghosts. But Raz did not seem to mind them, as he said, in a voice loud enough to be heard by all in the room:—

"I do most certainly believe in this one, though, and when you are done laughing, I want you to help me prove it to be no myth."

Surprise again overspread the countenance of the squire, but he did not reply, as all was instantly confusion, and all clamored to hear the story of the ghost. There was such a flow of jokes and witty

remarks that it was some time before anyone could
speak so as to be heard above the roar of voices.
At length a loud voice was heard calling them to
order, and saying that Squire Price would tell the
story if the people would be quiet enough to listen
to him.

"Hear! hear!" cried several voices, and the
squire repeated in substance what young Saunders
had told him. As soon as he had finished, confusion reigned again in the court room. At this
moment the door was closed between them and the
witnesses' waiting room, and Abbie saw no more.
But she had seen enough to understand her brother's intentions, and felt greatly relieved.

Squire Price soon joined Raz, and asked: "What
did you mean by asking me to prove that your
ghost was no myth? I don't understand you."

"I mean that that ghost was no other than Steve
Rushford, and I want you to help me prove it."

"But that cannot be, for I saw him in his cell not
an hour ago," said the squire in surprise.

"Nevertheless, I know he was at our place last
night," persisted Raz, in no way daunted by the
squire's skepticism.

"But how can we prove this?"

"I think it will be easy enough. That our visitor in white was no ghost I am sure, and that it
was Steven Rushford I am equally sure. Now it
follows that if he *was* there he must have escaped
in some way, and he never went through the key-

hole, that I know. Now it is my opinion that if we search we will find out how he made his escape."

"That's a good idea, Saunders. But if he did escape, what a fool he was for coming back!"

"Oh, he thinks he will get off scot free!" said Raz, as they neared the prison door.

The turnkey was at his post, and two or three gentlemen stood near.

"Is time up?" asked one of the gentlemen.

"Not quite," replied the squire. "I came to see if all's right here."

"All's right," spoke up the turnkey. "I guard this door, your honor."

"But Saunders says the prisoner was at his place last night between the hours of one and two. How do you account for that?"

"All bosh, sir!" and the turnkey bestowed a look of indignation and disdain upon young Saunders. "I locked him up myself at half past nine last night, and found him all right this morning. I should think that was plain enough proof for any man that he has not been out. He would be a fool to come back if he once got free."

"Are you satisfied?" asked the squire, turning to Raz.

"Yes," said Raz, with an undaunted look, "I am perfectly satisfied that I both saw him and heard him speak at our house last night between one and two."

"It must have been his ghost, then," said the turnkey, contemptuously.

"Perhaps it was," said Raz in much the same tone, "at least it was draped in white, although the voice was quite familiar."

"Saunders has seen a ghost," shouted several voices in a chorus, for by this time quite a crowd had assembled.

Raz paid no attention to the rabble, but urged the squire to search the cell. They entered and found Rushford apparently engaged in reading a book, which had been kindly furnished him to while away the tedious hours of his imprisonment. He rose with well-feigned astonishment, and greeted them.

Squire Price informed him of the accusation brought against him by young Saunders, at which he showed much surprise, declaring that, as they very well knew, he was locked in without the privilege of handling his own key, and that the story was absurd, and should receive no credence from sane men.

Then, turning to Raz, with a solemn and subdued air, he said: "Young man, if you have received a visit from the unknown world, I hope you will heed whatever warning you may have received, for it is a dreadful thing to disregard such warnings."

He looked at Raz with a bold, unflinching look, but as Raz still continued to hold his gaze, a look of confusion overspread his face, his eyes fell, and he turned away.

When he first began to speak, nearly all of his hearers believed him innocent of the charge brought

against him, but the last sentence opened their eyes.
Not a word had been said by Squire Price of any
warning, but only that he (Rushford) had been seen
there. His words proved that he knew more than
could possibly have been conveyed by Price's explanation, and they at once believed him guilty. This,
however, was yet to be proved, but it was not long
in being done.

As soon as he had lost Steve's eye, Raz set himself to work to discover the mode of his exit. He
could see no chance unless the lock had been
picked. The building in which Steve was confined,
and which was called the jail, was merely an old
dwelling house, and the cell was a small bedroom.
The window to this room had been barred, but only
the lock was used to secure the door, for, as the
turnkey slept in the next room on such occasions as
they had a prisoner (which was rare indeed), it was
considered sufficient. As soon, then, as Raz came
to this conclusion, he began to examine the lock,
and soon discovered that it had been lately removed.
He called the attention of Squire Price to it, and,
after examining it carefully, he pronounced Saunders' suspicions correct.

The murder was out. There was no use of any
further denial, and Steve was unmercifully bantered
and laughed at during the remainder of the day.
Had he owned it up when first confronted with the
accusation, it might have been treated more as a
joke, but in his attempts to deny all knowledge of

it, he had again overshot the mark, and exposed himself to the ridicule of all.   He sat among the laughing, shouting crowd, trying to put a bold face on the matter; but the ridicule of the crowd was too much, and he had to own himself beaten with his own weapons.   This was what Raz had intended, and he was satisfied.

They were soon called to the court room, and the business of the day commenced.   The witnesses for plaintiff were questioned and cross-questioned by defendant's counsel, but did not vary from their first statement, and were at length dismissed.   After several hours' wrangling among the lawyers, the case was decided in favor of the plaintiff.   Word to that effect was soon carried to Abbie, but she had scarcely time to rejoice before she was informed that defendant had appealed to a higher court, and that his counsel had gone bail for him, and he would be set at liberty.

The bail had been fixed at moderate figures, merely as a matter of form, for the authorities did not believe that bail could be found for him at any price, as he had few or no friends in the neighborhood except his counsel, and they did not believe he would go as far as that.   They were much chagrined, but it was too late to mend the matter, and he was released.   Taking the arm of his counsel, he walked out of the court room with evident exultation.

Captain Johns hastened to the presence of the

plaintiff. He was soon followed by Squire Price They did not like the turn affairs had taken, or the appearance of the defendant and his counsel, and felt sure that fresh annoyance, if not real trouble, was in store for their client. They blamed themselves for allowing bail, and hastened to do all they could to make amends by putting her on her guard against surprise in case any harm should be intended against her. They warned her to be cautious, and advised her father and brothers not to leave her unprotected for a single hour, cautioned her again about the child, and exacted a promise in case anything should happen that they should be informed of it immediately.

With heavy hearts Abbie and her friends started for home. They had not proceeded far, however, when they were hailed by one of a group of men who stood conversing near the road. He immediately came up to the sleigh and shook hands with Raz, saying:—

"That is a hard customer you have to deal with. Do you think you can cope with him?"

"We are three against one, and it is a pity if we are not a match for one man," said Raz.

"But you really have two of the worst men, to my thinking, that the country affords, to fight against," said the man, whom we will call Brown.

"You don't think Crosswell would stoop to help him in any of his deviltry, do you?" asked Raz, a shade of uneasiness in his voice.

"He may not really help him, for he is sharp enough to know that this place would be too hot to hold him pretty quick if he dared to do that," replied the man, "but he will help him plan his deviltry, which is about as bad, and instruct him how to act so as to give you all the trouble possible without really laying himself liable; and these gentlemen feel sure, as your lawyers do also, I think, that you have trouble ahead. We believe you will do as much as any man can to protect your sister, but if at any time you want any help, just let us know and we are on hand."

"Thank you," said Raz. "You are very kind, and I shall certainly call upon you if I need your help."

"Do so by all means, for I long to get a dab at the rascal."

Touching his cap, Brown rejoined his companions, while Mr. Saunders put whip to his horses, and away they sped toward home.

As we have before stated, a light snow had fallen during the night before, and now, as the sun, which was fast sinking in the west, threw its slanting rays across field and meadow, the scene was enchanting. Their road led across the river, then confined by the icy bands of winter; then out across the prairie, where cultivated fields, now lying idle and covered with snow, met their gaze on every side; past farmhouses, where children hastily scratched the frost from the windowpanes as they heard the bark of

the faithful watchdog, to get a glimpse of the passing sleigh, and where the patient cattle stood munching their dry hay, and shivering with cold; then
they plunged into the heavy timber that skirted the
river for a mile or two. Again crossing the river,
they emerged once more upon the open prairie, just
as the sun threw its last rays across hill and dale.
A brisk drive of half an hour brought them safe at
home.

Our heroine and her friends had only noticed the
beauties through which they passed in an absent
manner, and were glad to gather around their cheerful hearth once more. Scarcely a word had been
spoken by any of the party since leaving the village.
Each was too busy with his own thoughts to wish
to converse. And they had cause for deep thought,
for even as the shades of night had settled down
upon them as they entered the house, so the shadow
of coming trouble settled over that household.

Each had his own thoughts, and each kept them
to himself. Raz was by no means a coward, but he
began to feel the effect of this continual annoyance,
and was inclined to take severe measures in order
to rid himself of this trouble. He did not believe
that Steve would dare to do much if he knew they
were on the watch. It was the continual necessity
of this that chafed him. If this state of affairs
lasted much longer, it would necessitate the loss of
considerable money, as well as time, and they were
ill prepared for such an emergency. He was thank-

ful to Mr. Brown and his friends for their offer of
assistance, for he knew that a time might come
when he should need it.

Mr. and Mrs. Saunders were busy with their own
sad thoughts, and felt no inclination to converse,
so, after rather a dull evening, which was seldom to
be found in the sitting room of the Saunders family,
they retired to their rooms, and the house was soon
wrapped in silence.

We will now speak of Abbie, who had hardly
spoken since leaving the village. Those earnest
words of Squire Price, warning her to keep close
watch of her child, did not tend to reassure her,
and she clasped her darling tightly in her arms,
while her heart beat wildly with emotion, and hot
tears gushed from her eyes. She thought of its
being torn from her arms and borne far away, to be
nursed by strangers, perhaps neglected and abused,
and she felt that it would be more than she could
bear. She had been assured that, although the
custody of the child would undoubtedly be awarded
to her when all should be settled, yet, if he could
get possession of it, he might hide it away and thus
make her much trouble and cost in procuring it.

What pen can portray the anguish and fear that
filled the young mother's heart, as these terrible
possibilities passed through her mind. She had
not the assurance, that in some cases might have
lessened the sorrow, that it would be in the care of
a kind and indulgent father, who would shield it

11

from pain as far as possible. She knew that its feeble cries would be more likely to elicit anger than pity from that heart that should melt at its faintest tones of distress.

Alas, she knew but too well how hard that heart was! And yet she felt a kind of tender pity for him, and often wondered if no spark of love for his child ever tugged at his heart and begged him to relent.

Though she had watched, when in his presence, for one look of tender affection for his babe, she had seen only one of hatred and contempt, and she could but ask herself if it could be possible that he did not love his child.

The answer ever came by memories of his cruel treatment, and, clasping her child more tenderly to her heart, she prayed God to protect them both, and fell asleep.

When she awoke in the morning, the rest had somewhat relieved her fears, and she resumed her duty of assisting her mother, in a quiet, subdued manner, yet never for a moment losing sight of her child.

About three o'clock in the afternoon her little brother Eddie came in and said that Steve was at the gate and wished to see her. She started, turned pale, and bent an inquiring look upon her mother, who said: "He will not dare to harm you, my daughter. Do not give way so. Perhaps he only wishes to speak to you, and will then go away. It is best not to vex him if you can help it."

She had sprung and caught her babe, and now held its little soft cheek pressed to hers as she listened to her mother. Mrs. Saunders gently took the child from her arms, and bade her go.

"He may want to speak of some business matter," she continued, persuasively. "He seems quiet enough, and will give less trouble if treated well."

She was at last convinced, and, opening the door, she looked out. Steven Rushford stood leaning carelessly upon the gatepost, waiting for her. She turned a look full of tender love and fear toward her babe. Her mother understood and assured her that she should not pass from her arms until her mother's return.

Thus assured she passed out and up the footpath toward the gate. Steve watched her as she approached, and when at last she looked into his face, while her heart fluttered with fear, he bent upon her one of his old looks of exultation and malice combined, and she knew in a moment that he was again playing with her, and enjoying her look fo distress. The thought stung her almost to madness, and indignation took the place of fear. Fastening her eyes upon his face, she drew her form up to its full height, and stood, firm and defiant, before him, waiting for him to speak.

He gazed at her a moment in surprise. He had never seen that look in her face before, and could not understand it.

"Seems to me you are very high and mighty this morning," he said at last.

"Is that what you wished to speak about?" she asked in a cold tone, still keeping her eyes on his face.

Steve began to appear uneasy.

"No, no," he said in a confused manner, letting his eyes fall to the ground. "But you confused me with that strange look of yours. One would think," in an injured tone, "that you did not look upon me as a gentleman and worthy of respect," and he cast a furtive look toward her.

"Possibly I do not," was the reply, in an ironical tone, never removing her eyes from his face. She knew what that injured tone meant.

"I wanted so much to talk a little with you," he continued, still in a subdued manner that might have deceived even Abbie if she had not caught that first look, but now it only made her more firm and determined.

"Please be brief, then," she said, "for this keen air does not make standing here a very pleasant pastime."

"You are getting cold?" he asked eagerly. "Let us go in and sit by the fire," and he started to open the gate.

"No," said Abbie firmly, laying her hand upon the gate to prevent its being opened.

"How cruel you are," he said, in a disappointed tone, "and so careless of your own health, too! I really ought not to allow this in the mother of my only child."

"IS THAT WHAT YOU WISHED TO SPEAK ABOUT?"

He made another move to open the gate, but was arrested by her next words:—

"Oh, that makes no difference, as I may not live long anyway, you know!"

His face turned a vivid scarlet, and, turning on his heel, he stood a moment with his back toward her, then, turning toward her again, he said in a playful way:—

"Come, come, you must have been taking a dose of razors this morning, you cut me up so."

"It's a pity you did not take one too."

"What makes you so mighty sharp, anyhow?" he asked in a vexed tone. "I thought you never said nothing to nobody."

"There are certain schools of experience which tend to loosen one's tongue," she said bitterly; "but if you have nothing of more importance to say, I would rather be excused from further conversation."

Turning, she re-entered the house. When once there she took a woman's mode of relief from trouble, and burst into a violent fit of weeping. Soon controlling herself, she rose, and, wiping the tears from her eyes, while a hard, set look came into her face, she eagerly took the babe from her mother's arms and pressed it to her throbbing heart. An unnatural glitter came into her eyes, and a strange, almost wild look overspread her whole countenance.

Mrs. Saunders was pained and frightened at her manner, and in a soothing tone inquired what Rushford had wanted.

"He only wanted to see me that he might exult over me," said Abbie, in tones that were almost fierce. "As I came near him, he wore the same expression he used to wear when I had to set my teeth to keep from crying out under some cruel pain he was wantonly inflicting. I suppose he thought, because I came at his bidding, that I was the same submissive creature I used to be, but I think he has changed his mind by this time."

"Did he have no errand of any kind?"

"None at all. He merely commented upon my changed manner, and pretended to be very anxious to converse with me. He wanted to come in and sit by the fire while he talked, as he was very anxious about my health."

"But he has been forbidden to enter the house," interrupted Mrs. Saunders, with more asperity than was usual with her.

"He would never stop for that. The only reason why he seems to heed it now is because he knows he is watched. If he could get the least excuse, he would venture even now, but I don't think he will worry about my health any more right away. I think I have convinced him that I have a memory, though he seems to ignore the fact. I will give him as good as he sends, and meet him with the weapons he himself has furnished me, he can depend upon that," she added, her voice growing hard and determined.

Mrs. Saunders did not like this new turn in her

daughter's feelings. It did not agree with her idea
of feminine dependence, for she had been trained in a
school that had not one spark of the now-called
woman's rights in its make-up. So she said, rather
hesitatingly, "I don't think you had better see him
again."

Abbie looked up in surprise. "Dear mother,
what do you mean? I thought you approved of my
seeing him whenever he asked for me, and so perhaps ward off greater trouble."

"So I did. But if it has such a hardening effect
upon your heart, perhaps you had better not see him
again, and let things take their own course."

"You mistake my feelings entirely, dear mother,"
said Abbie in softer tones. "I am sorry I have given
way so. It was not ladylike in me, I must confess.
But you have taught me, my own sweet mother, to
be so quiet and submissive in all things, and I have
tried so hard (how hard you can never know) to
follow out your teachings that he takes my actions
to mean cowardice. You know he has asserted
that all this trouble has been caused by father's in-
terference, that I would not have made one word of
complaint, and that if he could get a chance to talk
to me he could persuade me to drop the whole
thing and go back to him. Now he knows that this
is false, but the world does not, and I have decided
that he shall never again have cause to say that I
am not allowed to see him whenever he asks for me
until all is settled. Then I shall drop him forever.

It is very unpleasant to be obliged to talk to him, but I will not let it appear that my father forbids me to see him and I dare not disobey. Besides, seeing him this morning has driven away half my fear and hesitancy, for that something terrible is coming I feel sure."

A shade of anxiety crept into her face, which a moment before glowed with firmness and resolution, and, bowing over her babe, which was sweetly sleeping on her lap, she almost smothered it with kisses. Mrs. Saunders looked on with a puzzled, pained expression; then, rising, she placed her hand upon her daughter's head, and, in tremulous tones, said:—

"My poor child, I will not oppose you in this your decision, but now is the time to use your motto. If you truly put your faith in God, he will not forsake you in the time of trouble. I have often wondered why this trouble has come upon us, but we must not murmur, my child. God's ways are not our ways, and it may be the time will come when we shall be able to see the hand of God even in this great affliction."

With these words she left the room.

Abbie sat for some time silent and subdued. She could not help looking over the occurrences of the morning, and asking herself if she had not trusted more in her own strength, during her conversation with Rushford, than in her God. Had her conduct been such that he would know that she had been and learned of Him?

Her conscious smote her; and, though she did not believe that she had been wrong in the theory she had advanced to her mother, yet she knew that, for the first time in her life, she had willfully given pain to another. Though the circumstances had been such as to seem to warrant her in what she had said, yet she knew that she had not done as she would be done by. She resolved to be more guarded in the future, and, remembering in whom her strength lay, she went to her own room, and, falling upon her knees, she asked her Father in heaven to help her bear her troubles in a Christian manner, to help her to stand firm for the right and eschew the wrong.

She rose from her knees strengthened and re-freshed, and when she entered the room where her mother was, it needed not words to tell from whence came that strength and peace which beamed from her countenance.

CHAPTER XIV.

TIME passed. Not a day went past in which she and her friends did not receive some annoyance from Rushford. He seemed to take delight in pouncing upon them in unexpected moments, and setting the house in a flutter, taking care, however, not to commit any act by which he might be again arrested, but vexing and worrying the family as much as possible.

One morning the family were awakened by hearing his voice, in faint and plaintive tones, calling: "Abbie, Abbie, O Abbie! have you no mercy in your heart for poor me? O Abbie, save me, your own Steven!"

The voice grew fainter and fainter until it died away in utter silence. Abbie, who had been awakened from sound slumber, was frightened and bewildered. She could not for a moment tell where she was; then, as her memory returned, she thought it must be a dream. Hardly had she come to this conclusion |before again was heard that low, plaintive voice, calling her name and begging:—

"Save me! O Abbie, save your own poor Steven!

(170)

Oh! shall I never see you again?" and again the voice died away.

In spite of the many deceptions that had been practiced upon her, she was now thoroughly frightened, and, springing from her bed, she flew to the window, and gazed eagerly out into the darkness.

At first she could discern nothing. The night was dark but not very cold. Snow covered the ground, and the first gleams of daylight were appearing in the east, casting a faint glimmer of light over the landscape.

She stood peering eagerly out into the darkness, when suddenly the cry was repeated. She started, and gazed more eagerly in the direction from which the sound came. Her eyes were becoming more accustomed to the darkness; besides, the light was growing stronger, and she soon caught sight of a dark object in the fence corner, on the opposite side of the road. She watched it until a slight movement, as if a hand had been raised then fallen again for want of strength, assured her that she had discovered the source of the plaintive cry,

All were now astir in the house. A light gleamed from the lower window, and she could hear the voices of her father and brothers as they discussed the probable cause of the strange disturbance.

"Looks as if he had come out there to freeze to death," said Will in his comical way.

"Took a strange time to do it, then," replied Raz. "I don't believe it would freeze a toad this morning."

"Seems to feel very bad about it, to judge by the noise he makes," continued Will, still gazing out of the window at the dark object in the fence corner.

"Perhaps he is freezing," said Raz doubtfully.

"It would be rather hard to let him freeze before our very eyes. Let's go and see."

"I don't think you had better," said Mr. Saunders. "Depend upon it, this is another foolish farce. He is not in any danger of freezing, but if you should go to him he would no doubt feign to be dead, so that you might bring him in, and so he gain admittance to the house. You had better wait a while longer."

From her window above, where she could plainly see every motion of the object of interest, Abbie had noticed that after the light appeared below, the voice across the way had rapidly sunk to a faint murmur. Then for a few moments all was still. So long did the time seem to her that she began to fear that all was over.

Her heart beat wildly, and she was about to fly to the room below and beg her brothers to go to his assistance, when there was a slight movement; the head was cautiously raised, and the man turned a quick look toward the house, then resumed his former position. The movement was slight, and only for a moment, but it was sufficient to show her that the object of her solicitude, so far from being dead, as she had feared, was on the alert, and watching the house as closely as possible.

She breathed a sigh of relief and began to notice the surroundings more particularly. She noticed that the form was lying upon a bed of fresh hay, which she knew did not lie in that particular corner the night before. If his object had been, as she had often read in novels, to die as near his beloved wife and child as possible, he had certainly been very thoughtful of his clothes. She also noticed that he had on a heavy overcoat, was muffled up almost to the eyes, and wore heavy overshoes, which he must have borrowed for the occasion. If he had come out there to freeze, he certainly meant to keep warm during the process.

After becoming thoroughly satisfied that another farce was being played, she turned to her babe, which, awakened by her hasty movement, had been nestling and grunting, turning its little head one way and another, trying to find its usual solace, but who, grown impatient at its want of success, was now expressing its indignation at such treatment by crying lustily. Abbie performed a hasty toilet, and, taking the child in her arms, descended to the room below, where she joined her brothers, who looked amused though somewhat anxious.

"Have you seen the show?" asked Raz with rather a sickly smile.

"Oh, yes!" said Abbie, returning the smile with interest and looking very much as though she would like to laugh outright.

"It doesn't seem to grieve you much," said he

surprised at her evident amusement. He had expected to see her frightened, and to hear her beg them to go to his assistance. He forgot that she was much better acquainted with the man they had to deal with than he could well be.

"Well, you see," said she in a tone of apology, "it seems so ludicrous for a man to borrow clothes to freeze to death in that I can't help laughing."

"What do you mean?" asked Raz, more astonished than ever, for from the window below they could not see him plainly enough to notice these things.

"I mean that he is muffled up to the eyes, besides having on a heavy overcoat and overshoes, which I am sure he does not own, to say nothing of having a fresh bed of hay to lie upon."

The boys did not wait for her to finish but sprang up the stairs and hastened to the window. It was broad daylight and every object could be distinctly seen. Sure enough, Abbie. was right. As the ludicrous performance became clear to their minds, they burst into a hearty fit of laughter, which made the house ring. They thought they saw the form in the fence corner move uneasily, as the sound floated out on the clear morning air, but all was instantly quiet again, and they returned to the room below.

"Did you ever hear of such a performance?" asked Will as they entered the room. "What do you suppose is his object?"

"His object is plain enough," said Raz. "He hoped to be brought in and nursed to life as they do in storybooks," opening the door and looking out. "I have a great mind to give him a good horse-whipping for his impudence."

"He would be apt to feel about as much of that as of the cold," said Will laughing.

They then went about their morning work, but kept close watch of the form in the fence corner, which by no means seemed to like its present position. Soon a hand was raised; then a foot was moved to a different angle; then he raised his head as if just awakening from sleep; then he rose, and, supporting himself upon one elbow, stared wildly around, as if in surprise; then he got upon his hands and knees and crawled a few steps; finally he rose to his feet, and, with tottering steps, started toward Mr. Deering's.

He played his part so well that the hearts of the watchers began to beat quicker, fearing lest he had really been suffering. They suspended their work and watched him with keen interest, as he stumbled along, as if he could neither see nor feel.

He did not seem to notice them, but continued to stumble, rather than walk, on his way. When he had traversed nearly half of the distance, he seemed to lose his way, and turned up the ravine, and at last stumbled and fell, just as he was entering a small grove, and did not get up again. They had all watched him with increasing interest up to this

moment, when Will, with his characteristic enthu-
siasm, exclaimed, "Whew, I can't stand that!" and,
bounding lightly over the snow, he was soon by
the side of the fallen man, who slowly rose to a sitting posture as he came up, and again stared wildly
around, as if perfectly bewildered.

"What are you doing here?" asked Will in a
gentle tone, for he never could kick a man when he
was down.

Steve cast a quick, furtive glance at him, which
puzzled Will greatly, especially when it soon disappeared, and a dull, expressionless stare took its
place.

Will was surprised into a moment's silence, then,
offering his hand, he drew Steve, with great difficulty, to his feet, and, supporting him, led him toward Mr. Deering's house. He leaned so heavily
upon him that it was as much as Will could do to
bear his weight, and he was much surprised, on
nearing Mr. Deering's house, to see him step from
his side with a firm tread, and, after giving him a
look which Will afterwards said made him "mad all
over," stalk boldly up the hill and into the house.

Will, crestfallen, retraced his steps toward home,
amid shouts of laughter from Raz and Joe, accompanied by some pretty loud smiles from Abbie and
Roxy, who had witnessed the whole scene.

"Why didn't you help him the rest of the way?"
called Raz, as Will drew near. "You are a pretty
fellow to leave a poor man in such a helpless condition to climb the hill alone."

Will came up to where they stood, looked at one and then another with that queer, comical look he always assumed when he had to acknowledge himself beaten, then with the one word, "Sold!" he passed them and entered the house.

Raz and Abbie looked at one another a moment in silence, then Raz said: "I hardly think Will is the only one that might cry, 'Sold!' I would not have believed the man capable of such a thing."

"I knew him to be capable of almost anything," said Abbie, "yet even I was frightened when he fell like a log and did not rise again. But let us go in, Roxy. We are not used to improving our health after this fashion."

So saying they entered the house, where Will was recounting his adventure to his father and mother, interspersed with the comical expressions and grotesque actions by which he always managed to shield himself from ridicule.

"If you had seen me," he said, "as I tugged his great form along, while he hardly used his feet at all, and did not seem to care which way he went, you might have felt like laughing at my grotesque appearance, but you surely would have thought, as I did, that his feet were frozen and his brain benumbed. He almost pitched me head first into the snow several times, and when he raised himself from my shoulder, I thought sure he was going to pitch into the snow on the other side of the road. But, instead, he straightened up and gave me a

12

look such as I cannot explain, but which told me as plain as words could tell that I was 'sold.'"

"If he had not seen you all watching," said Mr. Saunders, "he would have gone home at once."

"I suppose so, but he can't fool me again, that's certain."

"I don't know about that, brother," said Abbie. "I have seen him act a great many times, yet somehow I always think that this time it may be real."

"You might have known, all of you, that a man could not freeze such a morning as this," said Mr. Saunders, as he drew his chair nearer the fire.

Will and Abbie looked at each other with a meaning smile. They no doubt thought there was some difference between sitting by the fire in a warm room and lying in the fence corner. But if they did, they did not think it prudent to say so, and breakfast being pronounced ready, all repaired to the kitchen, which also served for dining room. They were soon seated around the table, where the events of the morning were freely discussed.

"It annoys me to see that man play the fool in this style," said Raz, after they had been talking some time. If he would come up like a man and fight for what he wants, it would not be so disagreeable."

"It might be more fatal, at least," said his mother. "I do hope this trouble may be got through with without shedding blood."

Raz did not look as if he shared her sentiments He was getting heartily tired of this child's play,

but he was doomed to bear a little longer, for hardly
had they begun the day's work before Rushford
walked up to the gate (which he had never pre-
sumed to pass since the shooting affair) with a firm
step and unconscious air, and asked if he might be
permitted to speak with Abbie.

She was informed of his request, and, throwing a
shawl over her head, she stepped out and walked
toward him.   He was now dressed with neatness
and care, presenting a far different appearance from
that of the morning.

"Good-morning," he said, as she approached.

"Good-morning," she replied, looking full in his
face.

"How are you," he continued.

"Well, thank you," in the same quiet tone.

He seemed at a loss what to say next, and she
continued:—

"Have you anything special to say to me this
morning?"

"Are you in any special hurry?" asked he in an
aggravating tone.   "If you are, we might just step
into the house, and then you could resume the
pleasant occupation of nursing baby."

She was so angry at this speech that it was with
difficulty she could restrain herself.   But she answered quietly, as before: "That is indeed a pleasant
occupation to me, but it would not be so pleasant
with you looking on; so please say your say as
quickly as possible, for my reception room is rather
chilly this morning."

She glanced past him at the pile of hay in the fence corner across the way. His eyes followed hers, then, turning quickly, he looked into her face, which was lit up with an amused smile. A flush of either anger or shame, she could not tell which, crossed his face.

Then, in tones of assumed tenderness, he said: "O Abbie, are we then parted forever? Is there not one spark of love left in your heart for me?"

He paused. She was standing full before him now, her shawl thrown back, while the winter sun shone over brow and hair, her thin cheeks glowing from the cool winter air, and her brown eyes, which were fixed full upon his face, wearing something of that look which he had often seen there in former days, yet with a mixture of something else he could not understand. He thought she had never looked so beautiful before, and moved a step nearer, but she recoiled as if from a serpent.

"Do you dare speak to me of love?" she cried, panting as if for breath. "You who never knew the meaning of that sacred word. You who, when I was most dependent on you for the natural fruits of love, gloried rather in inflicting pain; who could leave me helpless and alone for the most flimsy excuse; who knew no tenderer way to show your great love for me than to threaten my life and that of my child. I have consented to come at your beck and call, because I wished to give you fair play. But look you, if this subject is mentioned

again, it will prove our last interview, for I neither
can nor will bear this from you. I fear and loathe
you as I would a serpent."

Then she continued in a calmer tone: "Do you
suppose that your recent actions have tended to
augment my respect for you? A man who will
stoop to wrap in white sheets and play the ghost,
or lie in fence corners to elicit sympathy, is rather
to be pitied than respected."

"What do you mean?" he asked, in feigned surprise. "Have you been seeing ghosts?"

He did not seem to notice her vehement tone or
stinging words, but, after the first look of surprise,
stood calmly waiting till she was done.

"Yes," said she, "I have seen a ghost. But it
surprises me that you should try to deceive me in
this way. Have I been so superstitious that you
thought that your best hold on me?"

"I do not understand you," he said blandly. "I
cannot think what you are driving at. You seem to
talk in riddles this morning."

"Do you pretend to tell me that you know nothing of the ghost?"

"I most certainly do."

She looked at him incredulously. "Perhaps you
know nothing of lying in the fence corner, either."

"I most certainly do not," in the same tone. "I
know nothing of any such transaction, and I cannot comprehend why you should speak so to me."

She said no more. What was the use of trying

to reason with or show this man, who had neither truth nor honor in his make-up? She realized more than ever the utter depravity of the man. She had spoken words to him which should have brought a blush of shame, at least, to his face, yet he had not seemed to hear them. He had positively denied facts of which he could but be cognizant.

She again asked him his object in calling, and, receiving no satisfactory answer, she left him and entered the house. Then, as she thought over the conversation, she felt that it was mere nonsense to endure this persecution; that she must either rebel or suffer continual annoyance. Yet what could she do to escape it? If she refused to see him, it would tend to strengthen the report that she was not allowed to see him.

Something seemed to whisper to her, "Be true to yourself, and trust in God," and she decided to obey the voice hereafter. So when he again called for her, she refused to see him.

Perhaps the reader will wonder that she should see him at all, but they must know that Abbie was not in a position to either know or exact her rights, for several reasons.

Firstly, she or her relatives knew little of the requirements or privileges of law, having never been in a position to need its special protection before; and, secondly, they were in a new country, surrounded by men from all parts of the world, who had no special interest in one another, and who, like Deering, enjoyed the excitement that this family brawl, as they called it, furnished, little thinking or caring for the pain it cost at least one of the party. They would, had he committed any act of violence, have turned out to a man to punish him, but while, as they said, he did no particular harm, they let him go to furnish sport for them.

Abbie's legal advisers were so far away that she had not seen them except upon the three or four occasions when she had been called to town, so she did not know that it would be much better not to speak to him at all. She only knew that she hoped by seeing him to screen her father from blame, and perhaps save a collision between him and her brothers. So, although the decision at which she had so slowly arrived at was the one she should have adopted at once, it took considerable determination to adopt it, but having once decided she carried it out with firmness.

And she had need of firmness, for not a day passed that he did not call, and, upon being refused, walk up and down the road, and if this did not attract attention enough, sing songs or make speeches accompanied by ludicrous performances.

This caused much gossip in the neighborhood. Some said that he was a fool, and others that he must be crazy. This continued for some days, then all at once he disappeared, and Abbie and her friends breathed freely once more. Rumors were abroad hat a mob of men from the surrounding country had waited upon the gentleman and informed him that to their mind this had gone on long enough, that his room would be preferable to his company, and that he would greatly oblige them by leaving the country at once.

However, be this as it may, he was gone.

CHAPTER XV.

FOR some three weeks the family lived in peace. At about that time Anda drove up to the door and told them that his wife had sent for Abbie. She heard him from the door, and felt a thrill of pleasure, which was followed by such a sickening sense of fear that she turned from the door without even answering his salutation, and sank into a chair. Anda followed her, and, sitting down by her side, repeated the invitation, adding, " I must not take no for an answer, for Clara says I can have no supper unless I bring you."

Still she did not speak, and all noticed that her face was pale, and that she trembled with emotion.

"Why, sister," exclaimed Anda, "what is the matter? You are not afraid of me, I hope."

She smiled as if ashamed of her own conduct, and said quickly, "Oh, no! nothing could give me more pleasure, and yet—" and she hesitated as if undecided whether to speak or keep silent.

"Yet what?" said Mrs. Saunders and Anda in a breath.

"I don't just know," she answered thoughtfully.

(185)

"I seemed to feel such a pleasure as I heard your errand, then such a feeling of fear and dread followed as I cannot express. Something seems to say to me, 'Don't go, don't go!'"

Both looked at her in surprise. At length her mother said: "Pshaw! you are only nervous. You have been shut up in the house so long that I really think it will do you good to go. So put aside your foolish fears and go along."

"You don't want me to go to bed without my supper, do you?" said Anda, in a playful tone. "You might have some pity on me, at least."

"You don't look as if you needed much pity in that direction," said Abbie, trying to smile. "I should judge by your looks that such punishments had not been very frequent in your case."

Anda laughed, and said: "But, seriously now, sister, say you will go. We shall be much disappointed if you do not."

She allowed herself to be persuaded, although several times before she was ready she was on the point of giving up. She went, however, and was soon sitting in her brother's small but pleasant room, talking to her sister-in-law, of whom she was very fond. They had not seen each other for some time, and were not disposed to let the time go to waste now they were together.

Clara had a baby some five months older than Abbie's, and as Abbie had not seen it for some time, she was not quickly wearied of praising its bright eyes, its dimpled cheeks, and rosy mouth, which praise was received in good faith by the proud young mother, and the compliment returned in like praise of the little Ella, who only answered them by turning her great wondering eyes on her aunt, much as she would have done on any object that attracted her attention.

The little Lucy had lost all her first shyness long before tea, and had taken a decided fancy to her Aunt Abbie, who immediately appointed herself nurse of both children while she stayed, which her brother and sister had declared should be for several weeks.

Tea was soon pronounced ready, though how it had been prepared amid the flutter and confusion of Abbie's arrival can hardly be told. It was a happy group that sat around the table that night. Abbie had almost forgotten her fears at leaving home, and was enjoying her visit very much.

Scarcely had they left the table when the door was gently opened, and Lizzie, Clara's younger sister, came in, followed by several young girls who were schoolmates of hers, and who had accompanied her home to tea, with the promise that she and her brother, a young man of twenty, should accompany them to a protracted meeting which was being held in the neighborhood, and in which the young people were much interested. On hearing of Abbie's arrival they at once decided that she should go with them, and had come in a body to obtain her promise.

She at once decided not to go. She had not
attended a public gathering of any sort since her
trouble began, except in the court room, and the
disagreeable sensations then produced had not left
her. She pictured to herself the eyes of the gaping
crowd fixed upon her, and she shrank from it in
timid fear. The question was not so easily settled,
however. The girls were old friends. They loved
her and sympathized with her in her afflictions, and
were determined she should not drop out of society
for what was no fault of hers.

"Now, Abbie," said Lizzie coaxingly, "you surely
will not disappoint us. Say you will go. Clara
wants to go I know, and you know she cannot if
you refuse."

Clara gave Lizzie a deprecating look, and said
quickly:—

"I do not care to go this evening, so please yourself. I shall enjoy an evening at home with you, I
am sure."

"She only says that for manner's sake," said
Lizzie, who was an impulsive girl, and who, seeing
the doubtful look on Abbie's face, did not mean to
lose her advantage. "She 'most always goes, and
the new preacher is to be there to-night, so I know
she wants to go."

"Do go," said Rose Turner. "You ought not to
stay away from church, you know. The minister
said last night that the church was the best place
in the world for anyone in trouble."

"And I know you will like the new minister," urged Jane Corbit. "I met him at Aunt Janie's at noon, and he is just splendid."

"I would not stay at home and make a nun of myself for any man," snapped Betsy Green.

"Nor I either."

"Say you will go," again pleaded Lizzie, who never could give up anything she had set her heart upon.

She was undecided. She believed her sister would like to go, and did not like to stand in the way, besides, she really longed to go herself. She dearly loved the house of God. So, turning to Clara, she said, "I will go if you will."

"But do you really wish to go?"

"Yes, I think I shall enjoy myself very much."

"So you will go," cried Lizzie. "I knew you would. Now, girls, you promised to help me do up the work, you know, and it is time to be at it, for I must not leave anything for mother to do."

Away they went, and were soon at work. Willing hands make light work, and leaving them we will return to Clara and Abbie, who were also busy.

Clara was bustling about doing untold little household things, for who ever heard of a woman leaving home, even for a few hours, without an hour's bustle of putting things to rights?

Abbie washed, brushed, and dressed the little Lucy, who bore it all with a heroism that called forth loud praises from her aunt, who, when she had tied the last bow, held her up to look at her, and pronounced her the sweetest darling in the world. The fond mother said nothing, but, snatching a kiss from its rosy mouth, continued her preparations.

By the time the large old-fashioned sleigh drove up to the door, all were ready, and, seating themselves upon the fresh hay, they covered up closely with robes, and were prepared to resist Jack Frost for a much longer ride than they then contemplated.

The driver put whip to his horses and away they flew over the snow, the merry jingling of the bells keeping time to the clatter of the horses' hoofs as they sped swiftly along. They reached their destination, and were soon seated among the crowd.

The evening passed off much as usual in such places. Abbie enjoyed it very much, and was inclined to think that her friends were right in their new preacher.

When Abbie was again alone, she thought over the transactions of the day, as was her custom. She remembered her fear at leaving home, her ride over the snow, which she had hardly taken time to enjoy in her feverish haste to be at her journey's end. She thought of all that had happened since her arrival, and wondered that she had been so happy. It was indeed the happiest day she had passed for many weeks. And it was also the happiest for many weeks to come.

The next morning an invitation was received by

Clara from her mother, Mrs. Thomas, for her and
Abbie to spend the day with her. Accordingly, at
an early hour they set out, and were soon seated
in her large old-fashioned room. This room was
about twenty-five feet long by twenty wide. It
served for kitchen, parlor, and bedroom combined.
A row of beds ran across one side of the room.
These were surrounded by heavy old-fashioned
curtains, reaching from the ceiling to the floor. A
large cook stove with elevated oven stood near the
middle of the room, looking much as if it had
grown there. In all the many years that Abbie
had visited that house, she never saw it moved, even
an inch, from its accustomed place. It had stood
there immovable on the old kitchen floor until
the soft wood of which the floor was made had
worn away, leaving the stove legs upon small em-
inences resembling miniature mountains. This
served as a partition between the common work
room and the old lady's sitting room.

To-day Mrs. Thomas had brought out the old
cradle which had done service for Clara and all the
other young Thomases, and which, though her
youngest was then six years old, had never been
dismissed from the house, but occupied an obscure
corner of the great room, ready at a moment's
notice to be pressed into service. And it was not
idle to-day.

Mrs. Thomas, who, unlike most mothers, never did
housework when any of the girls were at home, sat

serenely knitting, while Clara bustled about to prepare dinner, and Abbie was perfectly happy in possession of both babies.

"Why, how motherly you look!" said Clara laughing. "You ought to put them both in the cradle and borrow mother's knitting. Then the picture would be complete."

"Thank you," said Abbie. "But mother loves her knitting best, while I love babies best; so you see we are both satisfied."

Abbie had not felt so happy and secure for a long time. She had almost forgotten that there was trouble in the world, or that she had aught to do but be happy.

But we must bid adieu to this happy home and see if we can ascertain the cause of Rushford's absence.

CHAPTER XVI.

RUSHFORD'S PLOTS.

PON receiving his visitors that night, and hearing their errand, he had immediately called upon his attorney, and, telling a tale to best suit his fancy, asked for his advice as to his future course.

"Well, what do you wish to do?" asked Crosswell. "You have not been successful, it seems, in persuading your wife to withdraw her suit."

"No," said Steve, with a despondent air, "I have been able to do nothing with her. The fact is, she is so set up by her folks that she will hardly give me a word. I feel perfectly sure if it was not for their influence, I could easily persuade her. Why, you have no idea what a tractable creature she is. She would obey me like a child. And so she will them, while she is with them. Confound it!" he continued in an excited tone, rising and pacing the floor, a look of demoniac rage taking possession of his face, "what a fool I was to tempt her. I might have known," he muttered between his set teeth, "that I could not tempt her if she did not think it right, and that if she did think it right I

13   (193)

could not stop her. She is stubborn as a mule where duty is concerned. 'Twas the knowledge of this that made me long to make her act contrary to her convictions for once. Fool that I was!" and he ground his teeth with rage.

Crosswell sat furtively watching him, as he paced up and down, his lips sometimes moving, though no sound escaped them. He did not exactly like his strange client; he felt sure that he had not been told the whole truth, and would have thrown up the case at once but that his motto was to succeed in whatever he undertook, whether right or wrong.

As Rushford made a short turn at the opposite side of the room, he met the eyes of his attorney fixed upon him. For a moment they gazed into one another's eyes. Crosswell's look was keen and searching, while Rushford's eyes quailed, and he let them fall to the floor, then, suddenly collecting himself, he crossed the room, and, sitting down, gazed fixedly into the fire. The expression of his face gradually changed, and when he again looked up his eyes were moist, and his face wore a beseeching look, as he said:—

"O Crosswell, you must help me!"

"Help you do what?" asked Crosswell with his characteristic smile. "Do you wish to break the neck of that little wife of yours?"

Steve hardly knew what answer to make to such a question, and as he hesitated Crosswell continued: "You look fierce enough for anything just now.

But perhaps that was not what you were thinking of."

"No, indeed," said Steve, somewhat relieved. "But I say, Crosswell, you must help me get her."

"Of what use will it be? She would only give you trouble."

"What do you mean? You don't mean to give up the case, do you?"

"I don't really like to, but then, you see, she has it all in her favor, and if you can't get her to change her mind, what's the use of more cost?"

"Oh, now," said Steve in an injured tone, "you know everything I owned in the world is in your hands, and it's too bad to leave a fellow in the lurch!"

"I haven't said I was going to leave you, have I?" said Crosswell. "I have no idea of doing any such thing. But it's pretty hard to sit still and see everything going against a fellow. I don't think you have been hardly fair with me from the beginning."

"Why not?" asked Steve uneasily. He did not quite like Crosswell's manner to-night. "Have I not given you every last cent's worth of property I had in the world? Haven't I obeyed you like a child?"

"Oh, yes," said Crosswell with a sneer, "you have certainly been childlike enough. But as to property, I think the less we say about it the better. It is poor enough pay for what I have done, to say nothing about what is to come. You know I am doing this job more to help you than to make money."

"I wish I could earn a team and wagon as easily," said Steve doggedly.

"Well, well, we won't quarrel about that. I have no idea of giving up the case. I would rather be beat than do that. But as we do not want to be beat, we must do something to turn the tables in our favor."

At this assurance the sullen, fierce expression on Rushford's face softened. He had begun to think that Crosswell meant to give up the case, and he was already planning a revenge. Crosswell had carefully scanned his face and had come to the conclusion that his client would be easier coaxed than driven. In other words, if he wished to control him, it must be rather through cunning and flattery than by force.

He now continued: "You know as well as I do that as matters now stand she is sure to gain the suit. Every item of testimony is in her favor. Besides, the whole town and neighborhood are up in arms and ready to fight for her. I have thought of trying the insanity dodge, but it won't work, I am sure, so had better be let alone. Now, the fact is we have got to do something to turn the tables in our favor, or we are sure to lose the suit. And what that something is to be seems to me to be the most important question just now."

He looked keenly at Rushford, who had sat watching him with a half-sullen, half-eager look as he talked, and who now started up and said, "Well?"

"Well," echoed Crosswell coolly.

Steve, who was not in the best humor in the world, was annoyed at this, and continued savagely, "Well, how do you propose to settle this important question?"

"I had a plan before you came," said Crosswell hesitatingly, "but perhaps it would not be best"—

He paused as if considering the subject. Rushford waited impatiently a few minutes, and then asked, "And what is your plan, and why will it not work?"

"I did not say it would not work," replied Crosswell with provoking coolness. "I think it is the only plan that will work."

"Then what more do you want?"

"Well, the fact is," continued Crosswell, still in that slow, hesitating way that irritated his client so much, "I thought my plan a brilliant one until you came, but now I feel somewhat unsettled concerning the propriety of the move. I fear it will not be best."

"But why will it not be best?" cried Rushford, vexed at these to him unintelligible words. "And what is your plan. Out with it. I am ready for any proposal that will help me get that girl again."

"And the precious babe," sneered Crosswell, looking him full in the face.

Rushford gave a sudden hitch in his chair and exclaimed: "Bother the baby! But then I suppose I shall have to take it if I do her."

Crosswell looked at him keenly. "I believe I lied

for you on that head about as strong as I ever did
for any man, and that's saying a good deal."

"Well, what is your plan?" again asked Steve.
" You can at least tell me that."

"I will on conditions."

"What conditions.   I am ready to make any conditions that will insure success."

"Too ready, I fear.   But that is neither here nor
there.   The conditions must be made in good faith,
for I am not willing to harm the little woman, even
to gain the suit, and if you do not love her, and
will not treat her well, the whole thing is better as
it is.   They call me a hard case, and perhaps I am,
but it goes mightily agin' the grain to plot against
a woman, especially when I know she is in the
right."

"Of course I love her," said Rushford.   " It don't
seem as if I could live without her.   As for my
former treatment, it was not fair, I'll own.   But I
have learned a lesson that I shall not soon forget,
and if you will help me get her, she shall be well
treated, I assure you."

"And you think she loves you and will be contented if once you get her away from her folks?"

"I do," said Rushford with more confidence in
his voice than he really felt.

"And you give me your word of honor that you
will treat her well?"

"I do."

"Then I will tell you my plan.   You know that,

according to law, a man has a right to full possession
of his wife and children, and whatever he may do
no man can take them from him unless she will
testify against him, and the law does not force her
to do this.   Now if you can get peaceable possession of her, and then persuade her not to appear
against you at the trial, you are all right.   I don't
see any other way to insure success."

"But how can this be accomplished?"

"You say you have friends in Wisconsin?"

"Yes."

"Do you think you could get some of them to
help you?"

"I think I could."

"They have teams, I suppose."

"Yes."

Still Crosswell hesitated to disclose his plan.   He
sat for some moments pondering over the matter,
and then said:—

"Yes, I think it will do.   Indeed, it is our only
plan of success, and it may succeed if you manage
it right, and do nothing by which they could snap
you up."

"Pray explain your plan, then," said Rushford,
rubbing his hands with satisfaction.

"Well, my plan is just this: You must go immediately to your old home, for there is no time to
lose.   This you can do in two or three days on
foot.   When once there you can tell such a tale as
will best suit your fancy, and if possible persuade

some of them to help you rescue your poor dis-
tracted wife from her cruel father. Procure a team
and driver, and return as soon and as secretly as
possible. Then watch your chance and get hold of
t he child. This they cannot force away from you
Then give your wife the choice between a life with
you in possession of her child or with her friends.
without it. My word for it, she will go with you,
and when you get her, if you cannot keep her then
you don't deserve to have her. If she goes, as I
feel sure she will, it will put a stop to the proceed-
ings of the court at present."

Rushford listened eagerly until he had finished,
then, springing up in excitement, he cried: "That is
just it. I'll do it, sure as guns. Give me your
hand, old boy. You're a regular brick after all.
Give me your hand, I say."

Grasping Crosswell's hand he shook it until he
called out to him to stop. Then, springing to the
middle of the floor, he danced and wriggled like a
madman; then, turning to Crosswell, who was again
beginning to feel that he did not understand his
client, he said apologetically: "I am so happy, old
fellow, you know. I feel as if I had got her and it
was all over."

"You never will get her if you don't control
yourself," said Crosswell shortly.

He might have added that he hoped he would
not, for the conviction was fast taking hold of him
that his client was a rascal. However, it was too

late to mend matters, so he said: "Where will you stay to-night? It is late to go to your boarding place. I might give you a bed here, but my wife does not like my being mixed up with your affairs, and might comb my hair for me."

"That would make a decided improvement in your looks," laughed Steve. "But I must decline the invitation, much good as it might do, for I could not sleep to-night. It would be simply impossible. I will start immediately on my journey. Good-night."

He walked out into the night and snow with a lighter heart than he carried when he entered the house of his counselor that evening. Hope filled his heart and lightened his step, as he thus began a journey of one hundred and fifty miles on foot, in the dead of night and the dead of winter.

Hope of what? that he might again press his wife and child to his breast, and shield them from care and sorrow?—No, but hope that he might triumph over those who were protecting them from his cruel power.

Such were his thoughts. But he felt that it would not do to tell his relatives the truth in regard to his trouble. He must concoct some story that would tend to make them sympathize with him, and also believe that Abbie was sorry she had left and would gladly come away with him.

Leaving him thus occupied we will return to the room he has just left.

As the door closed after his retreating form, Crosswell breathed a sigh of relief. But he did not feel so much relieved as he could wish. He knew that he had committed a dastardly act; that he was helping a bold, bad man.

"But what of that?" he asked himself, trying to still his troubled conscience. "Women often love and cling to their husbands when they are as badly treated."

He had known them to leave their husbands and fight them fiercely in court, then make up and seem as happy as ever. If Abbie Rushford was like these, the sooner she made up the better.

But this reasoning did not still his conscience, for he had a conscience, though he did not often listen to its still small voice. He thought of Abbie's sad, tearful face; of the gaze she fixed upon him when he was making his first plea; of the sad, hunted expression of those great brown eyes as she sat and heard him extol the virtues of his client; the wonder that was depicted on her face as he talked, making, as he knew, the white black and the black white; of the fire that seemed to burn in those orbs as he spoke of the tender husband and father deprived of the society of his wife and child.

He had known from that moment that she had not complained without a cause. Yet here he was helping her enemy plan mischief against her. He was angry at himself for what he had done, but it was now too late to mend matters.

He had felt, as he looked at Rushford, that it was a nefarious plan, and had resolved not to adopt it, yet he had been led on, by his own desire to conquer and the fair promises of his client, to divulge the plan. That it would be carried out if possible he was certain, and he retired that night much dissatisfied with himself.

CHAPTER XVII.

BUT Rushford did not know this. He pressed steadily on through the long, dark night, and when the sun cast its first rays over the earth, he was far on his way. Being hungry and weary, he stopped at a farmhouse and called for breakfast. This was provided, and, after refreshing himself and resting for an hour by the fire, he pressed on again. He had told the lady of the house a sad, pitiful story of misfortunes, and she had not only given him his breakfast but a luncheon also.

He traveled on in this manner until near home, when, finding that a brother lived near where he was, he decided to go to him for aid. This brother had known Abbie in Illinois and liked her very much. He had since married an old friend of the family, and when Steve told them that, owing to a trivial misunderstanding between him and her father, which grew into a family quarrel, she had gone home in a fit of anger, but had since been very sorry for her foolish act and was ready to come back if he would bring her away from them so there need be no more trouble, they sympathized

(204)

with him and were ready to do all they could to help him.

It was settled that in two or three days Steve would set out on his return, accompanied by his brother. He desired of his brother that, as it would be more pleasant for his wife when she came, they should say nothing of his trouble to any of their friends. To this both he and his wife agreed, and in their hearts thought their brother very thoughtful, and felt sure he must love his wife very dearly.

He talked pathetically of his babe, which he had hardly been permitted to see since its birth, and seemed so happy at thought of the reunion that they accepted his statement as true without question.

He visited his parents and sister, telling them he had decided to come and live among them, and that Bill was going with him after his wife in a few days, who was stopping at her father's. So smooth was his speech and manner that none suspected anything but unalloyed pleasure. He was cordially invited by his sister and her husband to make their house his home until he should see fit to settle in one of his own.

To this he gladly consented and promised to bring his wife there on her arrival.

This sister had early in life married a steady, industrious young man by the name of Harrison. He was a wheelwright by trade, and, being an honest, industrious man, had prospered in business and was now settled in a small village where his wife could enjoy the society of her relatives. He owned the house and lot where he lived, besides a commodious shop, and had a little money laid by for a rainy day. He was much respected by all his neighbors. His wife was an excellent housewife, a gentle, loving mother, who trained up her children in the way they should go, and was beloved by all who knew her.

Thus it was that Steven Rushford the more readily accepted her kind invitation because he trusted much in her influence to make Abbie consent to remain, for it must be remembered that he meant to bring her there against her will. Though he did not for a moment believe that his sister would consent to help him if she knew the true state of affairs, yet, trusting much in Abbie's submissive disposition, which had always yielded to him without demur, he hoped so to intimidate her before her arrival that she would not disclose the past. He expected her to be dissatisfied. But this he would charge to the score of homesickness, and thus induce his sister to use all her arts to make her contented with her lot. He had his plans well laid and felt sure of success.

But there was one thing that troubled him. He had not been straightforward and honest with his brother Bill. Instead of placing the facts before him, he had led him to believe that Abbie had no quarrel with him, but that, if the chance was offered, she would gladly leave her own people and cling to him.   He dared not even hint that this was not the case lest his brother should refuse his assistance. So he kept his own counsel, and in due time they were on the road.

The nearer they arrived to their destination the more Rushford's mind was troubled with doubts and fears.   His face wore a gloomy, troubled expression, which soon attracted the attention of his brother, who at once asked the cause.

"I fear that we shall fail at last," was the answer, in a despondent tone.

"Pshaw, cheer up, man!" laughed Bill.   "This weather is enough to make any man feel blue, I own, but you must not lose heart, old fellow.   Think how glad Abbie will be to see you again."

Rushford winced at this.   He well knew there would be more sorrow than joy at sight of him, but Bill must not know this until she was safe in his hands.   But how he was to accomplish his object without confiding in his brother was more than he could tell.   He had puzzled his brain in vain for an answer to this harassing question.   And now Bill was tired of this quiet way of riding, and seemed determined to better understand the errand they were on.

Noting Rushford's movement, he said, "You don't seem so sure of your reception being a warm one as I could wish."

"I fear it will be too warm for us," replied Rush-

ford, again shrugging his shoulders. But the har-
assed look left his face, and he smiled, or, rather,
grinned, at his brother, who sat looking at him in
astonishment. As Bill spoke, a bright idea struck
him, and he was himself again.

"What do you mean?" asked Bill. "You don't
expect any trouble, do you?"

"Not much, though the Saunderses will make
us trouble enough if they can get the chance."

"How so?"

"Well, you see they won't want Abbie to come,
of course, and will do all they can to hinder her.
They may go so far as to prevent her leaving the
house."

"I'll not help you in that scrape," said Bill, to
whom the idea of a fuss with other people was
unpleasant in the extreme. He was a lover of peace,
and often congratulated himself on having got so
far through the world without one downright fight.

When in some of the Eastern States he had fallen
in love, and become engaged to a lady of high position in society. But the father of the girl, not liking the match, forbade his daughter to see him.
This order she disobeyed by meeting him clandes-
tinely. The father, when he heard of this, was
greatly enraged, and, locking his daughter up in
her room, informed her lover of what he had done,
and coolly told him that the term of her imprisonment depended wholly upon him; that as soon as
positive proof was received that he was in a far
country, she would be set at liberty, but not before.

This was a trying position for a lover to occupy, and, to make matters worse, he received two or three notes, by means of the servants, from his imprisoned lady, full of protestations of her undying affection, and entreaties that he would effect her release.

Some of his young friends urged him to attempt this, offering their assistance. But this he refused to do, saying that if he got her in that way it must cause a lasting enmity between them and her family, and perhaps she herself would repent the move, and thus all become unhappy. Sitting down he wrote a letter to her father, stating his intentions, and another to her, bidding her a last farewell.

He came away bearing with him her letters, which, through a mischievous prank of a cousin of his, had been read in the hearing of Steve and Abbie two years before. If, then, he would not fight for his own love, it was hardly to be expected he would fight for another's.

"I think there need be no trouble," continued Steve. "I made an agreement with Abbie that will tell me how the land lies. If she shows herself boldly, I am all right. But if she does not, I must watch my chance. That is all."

"Very strange bargain, that is. Why don't she come along if she wants to. She need not think I am going to run my head into a hornets' nest to help her. If she hasn't got pluck enough to walk out to the gate, she isn't worth much; that's all

14

I've got to say." Bill gave his horses a cut across the flank that made them wonder who held the lines.

"I don't ask you to fight for her," said Steve, in a persuasive tone. "You just drive where I tell you, and I'll do the fighting."

"Yes, and you may for all of me."

"Come now, Bill, don't get in a huff. It will be all right, I think, and if she is slow I know how to fetch her."

"Indeed you do. How is that?"

"You see, I did not come off down here without knowing what I was about," continued Steve, in a confidential tone. "I have a friend up there, a lawyer, and when she refused to leave home until I brought a team to take her to my mother, I just went to him and asked for a little advice. You see I was pretty mad, but I did not want to do anything that would lay me liable to the law, for I knew those Saunderses would snap me up in a minute if they got a chance. Well, as I said, I went to see the lawyer and told him the whole thing as it stood. He advised me to come and get the team, then if she don't come to time just watch my chance and get the child. This he says they cannot touch me for if I use no force. Then just give the lady the choice between coming with me without any more fooling, or stay without her child. Now you know my plan in case she does not come to time; what do you say to it?"

"I say it is a mighty foolish plan, and if I had

known it before I started, it would have been some time before you got me up here. I don't like this idea of fighting for a woman no how. If they don't like a fellow well enough to stick by him, let them go, I say."

"Oh, now, Bill, don't get wrathy! There is the little one. I could not live without that, you know, old fellow, especially if it was being brought up by those Saunderses and taught to hate me, and all that, you know."

"Oh, yes, I know!" said Bill, somewhat mollified. "But suppose she will not come, and you can't get the child, and all that, you know?"

"Let me alone for that. I'll get the child fast enough, never you fear. Besides, they may forget their pet by the time we get there, and make no objections to her going. I would not wonder a bit if they did. However, we shall know in a short time, as we are almost there. If Abbie comes out to meet us, perhaps we will stop there all night. If not, we will drive on to the next house and put up."

"I suppose it is all right if you say so," said Bill, "but I can't see what makes Abbie such a fool. I thought she had more sense. She looked to me like a girl with an uncommon strong mind."

"So she is. And if I get her away from her father, she'll be all right again. You know he has a strong mind too, and Abbie has been used to obeying him, so when I got mad and abused him a little, she could not stand it. I suppose I ought not to have done it, but then I was mad, you know."

"Better hold your temper next time. I think that indulgence has cost you dear enough."

They drove on in silence again. Just as the sun was going down, they neared Mr. Saunders' house. But Steve suddenly remembered that they could not get through on that track, and must turn out and go round half a mile or so. He had no intention of being seen and recognized by Mr. Saunders that night. Bill did as he was directed, and when they again neared Saunders' place, it was too dark to be recognized. Of course they saw nothing of Abbie, and drove on to Deering's to put up.

Steve insisted upon helping Deering put up the team, while Bill took care of the luggage. When they were alone, Steve requested Deering not to speak of his trouble to his brother, as he (the brother) felt very sore on the subject, and would not like to speak of it with strangers.

Deering consented, but as soon as he was alone he muttered uneasily: "Mighty tender of his brother's feelings! I warrant that same brother don't know his errand any too well. I wonder what he is up to, anyway. Be hanged if I like his hanging around here. If I find he's up to any mischief, I'll let Saunders know."

But nothing was said that gave him any clue as to their intentions, and they soon retired.

In the morning, as soon as they had eaten their breakfast, they started out without giving a hint as to their destination. They drove to the village, where

Steve purchased a bottle, which on his way back he had filled with milk.

"For," said he, "we may have to keep the babe a few hours, and had better be prepared."

Then, learning that Mr. Saunders' men were at work in the timber, they drove boldly up to the gate, and, alighting, entered the house. Mrs. Saunders, who was engaged in some household work, started with surprise at their abrupt entrance, then, as she recognized her visitors, her face blanched with fear. She at once divined their errand, and felt a momentary relief that Abbie was not at home.

"Where is Abbie?" demanded Rushford roughly.

"I decline to answer your question," she answered firmly.

"Then I will soon find out."

He moved toward the door which led to the chamber, where a slight noise led him to think her concealed.

Mrs. Saunders quickly stepped before him, and said, "You must not pass that door."

"We'll see about that," and he seized her roughly by the arm, and, flinging her to one side, sprang through the door and ascended the stair. But instead of Abbie he encountered Roxy, busy at her chamber-work. He was somewhat taken back, for he felt sure of finding Abbie.

"Where is Abbie?" he again asked, but, receiving no more satisfactory answer, he proceeded to search the house, but without success. Then, returning to the room he had just left, he said: " I demand to be informed of the whereabouts of my wife. I have come to take her away, and you have no right to conceal her."

"I have not concealed her," Mrs. Saunders answered, " and I cannot tell you where she is."

" Do you mean that you do not know?"

"I did not say that."

" Then you know, but refuse to tell. Is that it?"

" It is."

"Then, be certain," cried he, in a loud and angry voice, " I will make you repent this! For look ye, I will not give up the search until she is found, and if I succeed in getting possession of her, she will pay for this."

" You won't get her," said Eddie, who stood by his mother's side, his little form drawn up to its full height, his eyes flashing, and his lips quivering with indignation. "Anda won't let"—

He was checked by a violent shake from his mother, and he turned and looked at her in surprise. She was pale and trembling with emotion, which she tried in vain to conceal.

The eyes of Bill and Steve were fixed upon her, and as Rushford noticed her emotion he at once divined the truth.

" So she is at Anda's, is she, my little man?" said he, with an exultant smile.

As he received no answer, he nodded to his brother, and they left the room, and, springing into

the sleigh, drove with all possible speed toward
Anda's.

"O my son, what have you done?" cried Mrs.
Saunders in an agony of grief, as she sank, weak and
exhausted, into a chair, while little Eddie, who now
saw his blunder, flung himself sobbing upon the
floor, and Roxy and the others stood by, dumb with
fear and astonishment.

Mrs. Saunders rose, and, tottering to the window,
looked far down the road. But nothing was to be
seen. Team and driver had long since disappeared.
Then, again sinking into a chair, she cried in her
helpless agony, "O God, protect my child!" And
who shall say that God did not hear and answer
that mother's wailing prayer.

But we must follow the movements of Steve and
Bill. They had started on the main traveled road
to Anda's. Neither spoke a word except as Steve
directed where to drive, until, as they entered the
woods, Steve ordered a halt.

"Well, what now?" asked Bill, who had not
spoken a word since entering Mr. Saunders' house.

His mind had been a strange mixture of thoughts.
He had felt angry and surprised at his brother's
manner of addressing Mrs. Saunders, and when he
laid his hands upon her, he felt like springing up
and defending her, but before he had time to do
this, his brother was half way up the stairs, and as
the search continued without meeting with any
success, he began to feel some interest in the issue.

Then, when little Eddie so boldly took up the defense, and in his childish ignorance disclosed the whereabouts of his sister, he was considerably amused. He began to lose his dislike of his position, and take an interest in his brother's success, which caused the foregoing expression.

Steve did not answer immediately, but seemed to be pondering over some puzzling question.

"I think we had better not take this road," he said at last. "It leads through the timber where the Saunderses are at work. They may see us, and if we don't want the whole pack of them down upon us, we had better avoid them. There is an old road leading across the slough that is much shorter. It probably is not broken now, but as the snow is not deep, I think we may venture."

"All right, you are the boss of the business," said Bill, as he turned the horses' heads in the direction indicated.

They again drove on in silence. They found, as Steve had predicted, that the road was not broken; but as the snow was not deep, they found no difficulty in traveling, and were soon within twenty rods of Anda's house. Here they were completely hidden from view by the heavy timber that surrounded the homestead of Mr. Thomas, and they stopped to hold a consultation with respect to their future course.

It was agreed that Steve should go to the house alone, and do what he could to induce Abbie to go

"ALL EYES WERE TURNED TOWARDS THE DOOR."

with him. As he would probably be gone some time, and as Bill did not relish the plan of sitting still in the cold, it was agreed that he should drive up and down the road. As it was an unfrequented road, and lay for the most part in the timber, there was not much danger that he would attract attention. It was also agreed that he should not go far enough but what he could hear a signal given by means of a shrill whistle which Steve carried in his pocket. When he heard this signal, he was to drive quickly toward it, and be ready to be off as soon as Steve reached the sleigh.

After all was settled, Steve walked on toward the house. Finding, on nearing it, that no one was at home, he passed on to the residence of Mr. Thomas. He was perfectly acquainted with the place, and, fearing he would be refused an entrance, he entered without ceremony.

Clara was standing by the table with her preparations for dinner. Anda was sitting by the fire. Abbie was sitting by the cradle in which her little Ella lay sleeping sweetly, while Lucy was resting in her arms.

As the door opened, all eyes were turned toward it. Clara stood rooted to the spot with fright, while Anda rose as if to intercept his entrance, but before he could make a move, Steve had entered and closed the door. Then, turning, he walked deliberately toward the fire. . Abbie was paralyzed with fear and sat for a moment powerless to move. But as he neared her, she suddenly remembered the advice of her counselor, and, springing to her feet, she handed the little Lucy to its father, and turned to take her own babe. But Steve had been too quick for her, and had lifted the sleeping child in his arms.

"Oh, give her to me!" pleaded Abbie, lifting her arms imploringly toward the child.

"Don't be in a hurry," said Steve, while an exultant smile lit up his evil countenance.

To Abbie he had never looked so terrible before, and, stepping forward, she took hold of the child, while she turned her eyes, full of intensest agony and entreaty, on his face, and pleaded, " O Steve, do give her to me!"

Anda stood by, undecided whether to interfere or not. Steve, seeing this, said, in a gentle, persuasive voice: " Don't be in a hurry, I want to take her a moment. I think you are very selfish. She belongs to me as well as you, and yet I have hardly seen her. Come, sit down. I want to talk to you."

He pushed her gently toward a chair. His gentle tone and manner somewhat mollified Anda, who was not so well acquainted with him as the others, while he fastened his baleful eyes upon Abbie's face, well knowing that she would understand their language. As she sank into a chair overcome with fear and emotion, he also sat down. But instead of noticing the child, he held it carelessly in his arms, while he kept his eyes fixed upon Abbie's face. The little one did not wake, but, suiting itself to its new position, slept on, all unconscious of the drama that was being played in its presence, or of the important part it was doomed to play.

It was a strange, thrilling picture—the large, old-fashioned room, with Clara standing immovable by the table, for she had hardly stirred since the entrance of Steve; Anda sitting in his chair, but ready to spring at a moment's notice; Mrs. Thomas, who in her fright had dropped her knitting, and sat looking at first one and then another; Abbie, pale and trembling, with her eyes fastened upon Steve, who still held her with his cruel gaze, the power of which she did not seem able to resist; the strong, wicked-faced man, equipped in his rough outer garments, and the tender babe, scarce two months old, resting upon his arm, its long muslin dress almost sweeping the floor, its shoulder blanket fallen down, and revealing its plump little arms and neck to view. They sat thus when Steve again spoke:—

"I am tired of living without my babe, and have concluded to take her home to my mother. If you have a spark of love for her, I hope you will conclude to go with us. I have a team in readiness, and you must decide at once whether you stay here without your child or go with it."

He paused a moment, but, receiving no answer, continued, "Once more, will you go?"

"No, never," said Abbie, who in that brief moment had made her decision.

She had read his purpose in his eye, but could

not believe he would execute it, and, well knowing what would be the fate of her and the child if she threw herself into his power, she determined to oppose him to the last, and trust in God for the issue.

"Is that your final decision?" he asked, still striving to intimidate her by his gaze.

"It is," she replied firmly.

He arose and began pacing the floor, still holding the unconscious form of the infant in his arms. Each time he crossed the room, he approached nearer the door. Once he paused as he approached it, and seemed to listen, then resumed his walk.

Divining his purpose, Abbie rose and placed herself against the door, while Anda took a position near by. Steve's face assumed a derisive smile as he noticed this movement. It would only necessitate a little more strategy on his part, and he continued his walk. He would approach so near Abbie that she could touch the child, then turn and walk to the farther end of the room, and again return to her.

This was a trying moment for Anda. He was a small man, very short of stature, and, besides, not enjoying his usual strength, having just recovered from a severe illness, while his tormentor was a large, powerful man, against whom his resistance would be but child's play.

This state of affairs was unendurable, however, and both made a move to secure the child, at which Steve drew back, and, taking the child by its feet,

made a move as if he would dash its head against
the wall. The brother and sister recoiled with horror at the sight, and, with the same demoniac smile,
he resumed his walk. At length, as he neared the
door, he made a sudden movement; dashing Abbie
to one side with a violence that made her reel, he
opened the door and was outside in a moment.

Anda sprang after him, and Abbie, recovering
from her shock, quickly followed; but she was just
in time to see him vault lightly over the low fence
that surrounded the yard, the babe on one arm, its
blanket still hanging by one corner, and its tender
white arms, neck, and head exposed to the cold,
piercing wind. As he sprang over the fence, he
uttered a shrill whistle, and suddenly disappeared
from sight in the dense woods, followed by Anda,
Raz, Will, and Deering, who had just appeared
upon the scene. They saw the team drive up, turning just as he reached it, into which he sprang, and,
catching the bottle of milk, enveloped himself and
the child in the blanket, and all instantly disappeared
in the distance and gloom of the woods.

Leaving them to pursue their flight, we will return and learn how it was that Raz, Will, and Deering appeared thus abruptly at this moment.

CHAPTER XVIII.

RUSHFORD KIDNAPS THE CHILD.

IT will be remembered that Deering did not quite like the appearance of his visitors, and had tried in vain to ascertain their business. After they had gone, he told his wife that he believed they were up to some mischief, and she begged him to inform Mr. Saunders of their presence in the neighborhood. This he refused to do, saying he would have nothing to do with it. He watched them drive to Mr. Saunders', and leave again, taking the wood road.

At last, curiosity getting the better of caution, he set out to ascertain, if possible, their destination. Just after entering the woods he perceived that they had left the wood road and crossed over to the old one. This excited his curiosity still more, and he followed them. He knew that he was not mistaken in the team, as he had noticed a peculiarity in one of the horses' feet, which was plainly visible in the track left in the snow.

He had not proceeded far when he saw the team slowly approaching. Hiding behind a large tree, he watched it as it approached, and, seeing that the

(222)

sleigh was occupied by Bill alone, and that he was moving slowly, as if waiting for someone, his interest was excited to the highest pitch. Bill soon turned and retraced his steps.

As soon as it was safe, Deering left his hiding-place, and, slinking through the woods, hastened to where Raz, Will, and Mr. Saunders were at work. He did not know that Abbie had left home, and could think of no reason for the strange behavior of the brothers except that Steve intended taking vengeance upon the Saunderses by hiding and shooting them while at their work.

The distance was considerable, and as his progress was greatly impeded by deep snow and underbrush, he was weary and panting for breath when he at last reached the spot. As he entered the clearing, all noticed his flushed face and quick breath.

"Why, Deering, what is the matter?" cried Raz, in sudden alarm. "You look as if you had been running for a wager."

"Come here, and I will tell you," replied Deering, seating himself near a large pile of wood, which effectually screened him from that part of the woods in which he supposed Steve to be.

The three men dropped their tools and were quickly by his side, for they knew that something of importance to them had happened.

Motioning them to be seated, Deering, in as few words as possible, told them what he had seen, and what his suspicions were.

"Did you say they were at the house?" asked Will in an eager tone, his face blanching.

He seemed to have anticipated the question of both the others, for they turned eagerly to Deering for the answer.

"Yes, I saw them both go in, but they soon came out and started in this direction."

"Can it be they have discovered the whereabouts of Abbie?" asked Raz in dismay.

"Where is she?"

"At Anda's."

"That's it!" cried Deering, springing to his feet, and forgetting his fear of the hidden foe. "I am sure of it now, for they had blankets, and everything to keep a woman warm."

But Raz did not hear the last part of his speech, for he had started off at the first hint of danger to his sister, and was far on his way, followed by Will, before Deering had finished speaking. Deering followed, with what result we have already seen.

Old Mr. Saunders, being thus left alone, hastened to hitch his team to the sleigh, and followed the others to the scene of action, where he arrived just as the boys returned from their fruitless chase and were entering the house.

Here a strange and heartrending scene met his view.

Old Mr. Thomas and his sons had come in, and all was in the wildest confusion, Raz and Will in their excitement blaming Anda for not shooting

Steve upon the spot, forgetting how often they had
let him escape unscathed; Mr. Thomas and his
sons vainly trying to find out what had happened;
Clara, pale with excitement and pity for Abbie,
walking up and down the room, trying to still the
little Lucy, who, frightened at the uproar, was crying lustily; Abbie, sometimes walking the floor and
wringing her hands, while piteous moans escaped
her lips, then, falling upon her knees at Mrs.
Thomas' feet, she would bury her head in her lap
and weep. Ever and anon she would raise her head,
and, gazing into the cradle from which her darling
had been taken, she would again hide her face and
weep as if her heart would break.

Other eyes were also dimmed with tears as they
followed hers. There, upon the pillow, was the
print of the baby head. The blanket that had covered it had been scarcely stirred by its removal.
Its cloak and hood lay upon the foot of the cradle
where they had been thrown upon entering the
room, while the babe who had worn them was exposed to the biting cold with no other covering save
the coarse blankets which were in the sleigh.

"Oh, why did he not take its cloak?" wailed the
poor mother, while tears streamed down her face.
Then, rising to her feet, she went to meet her father,
whom she had not seen until that moment.

"My poor child!" he said, as the tears flowed
down his aged face.

"Do not grieve so, dear father," she said, with a
great effort controlling her voice.

15

A strange fire burned in her eyes and she trembled violently, but few more tears were allowed to fall, though her face was as white as marble. She bent eagerly forward and listened.

Will Thomas was talking rapidly. He proposed that they collect six or eight men, follow the brothers, secure the babe, and mete out to the rascals the punishment they deserved. It was a shame, he said, for men to sit still and see a tender infant torn from its mother's arms, and borne away to suffer, perhaps to die.

Abbie's heart stood still with fear. She fully believed that Steve would never let them take the child alive, that any attempt to rescue it would be more likely to result in its death than its rescue. Just as they were agreed and prepared for action, they were startled by Abbie's voice, crying, in clear, shrill tones, "Stop, men; for the love of heaven, stop!"

All eyes were instantly turned upon her. There stood the woman whom they had seen wringing her hands in an agony of grief for her lost child. Now her eyes were no longer dimmed with tears, but filled with that strange fire which her father had remarked as she joined him. Her face was pale, her lips twitched nervously, and one hand was raised to command silence.

At length, in a clear, calm voice, she said: "I do not for a moment doubt your kind intentions, but, believe me, any attempt to rescue my babe by force will only result in failure, or what to me would be even worse, the recovery of its dead body. I know the man with whom you have to deal better than you do. While he has possession of the child, he will do the best he can for it, but he would now, in the heat of his passion, sooner take its life, which you would be powerless to prevent, than allow it to be taken from him."

"But, Abbie," said Raz, coming to her side, "we cannot sit still like cowards, while the child is being taken away."

"You cannot prevent it, my brother. I repeat, he will take the child's life before he will give her up."

"But he surely would not kill his own child!"

"I believe Abbie is right," said Anda. "I believe he would have dashed her brains out against the wall before our very eyes if we had not desisted in our attempt to take her before he left the house."

She gave her brother a grateful look, and waited impatiently for their decision.

Deering stepped forward and said: "Gentlemen, throughout this whole affair I have, as you all know, occupied the meanest position a man can hold, that which is designated as 'straddle of the fence.' I am heartily ashamed of myself, for I feel that I am to blame for this trouble. If I had done by my neighbor as I would have him do by me, I would have informed Mr. Saunders of the arrival of the villains in the place. This, however, I did not do, and that mother standing there, so white with anguish, yet so brave, might well curse me for the loss of her darling. I ask her forgiveness, and pledge myself to die, if need be, in the attempt to rescue her child."

A deathlike stillness reigned throughout the room, until Abbie stepped forward and shook him by the hand. All in the room followed her example, and another lasting friend was added to their already large list of friends.

It was thought best for Abbie to return home with her father, and they were soon upon the road. Will and Deering attended them to guard against surprise. Raz stayed behind, on some trivial excuse, and Abbie feared he had not abandoned the idea of an attempt to rescue the child.

With what a sad heart did she set out to return home! Just twenty-four hours before she had passed through these woods in peaceful possession of her child. Now she was returning, her arms empty, her heart aching, the little bundle of clothes lying in her lap being all that was left to her of her darling.

When they reached the gate, she alighted, and, passing up the familiar path, entered the house. She seemed in a daze, scarcely knowing where she was, until her mother caught her in her arms, and, kissing her pale brow, repeated those solemn words, "Trust in God, my child."

"Oh, I do, I do!" cried Abbie, bursting into

tears. But these were soon dried, and again that strange light shone from her eyes. She scarcely seemed to notice anyone, but roamed listlessly over the house, seeming in search of something, yet never uttering a word.

The news spread over the neighborhood like wildfire, and soon a large circle of friends waited upon the family, sympathizing in their bereavement, and offering their assistance. Abbie hardly saw them, but continued to roam here and there, until her mother, unable longer to endure the sight of such grief, entreated her to calm herself and partake of some refreshment, as she had eaten nothing since morning.

"O mother, I cannot!" she cried, again wringing her hands and weeping.

"But you must, my child," said her mother, in a firm but persuasive voice.

Abbie yielded without another word, but her mind was greatly agitated. She did not scream or make any violent demonstration. But, oh, the terrible pain gnawing at her heart! She felt sure that Raz, backed by Will Thomas, was bent upon raising assistance and pursuing the brothers. She knew that, in the then excited state of the neighborhood, scarcely a man would refuse to go. A large mob would be the result, which, with the clue they possessed by which they could track them through the snow, would be almost sure to result in the capture of the brothers.

She thought of her babe in the power of its cruel parent, of his anger and desperation at finding himself pursued, saw the pursuers gain upon him, and saw the demoniac light gleam from Rushford's eyes. Would he, oh, would he consummate his terrible revenge by raising his hand against his child. The picture was horrible in the extreme. She could not shake it off. She could not share it with others. She could only pray and trust. She hoped that if he were not molested, he would return the babe in a few days. But if angered by pursuit, all hope of such a result was gone, and she prayed, as only a bereaved mother can pray, that the pursuers might be confounded, and that her darling's life might be spared.

An assurance that her child would be spared, and that she could again press it to her heart, took possession of her soul. She rose from her knees, arranged her toilet, and, entering the kitchen, performed her usual duties of assisting her mother.

Mrs. Saunders was startled at this strange way of bearing grief, and feared her mind was giving way, but when, on conversing with her, Abbie told her of her faith in the answer to her prayer, and she had looked into those firm, trusting eyes, she felt no more fear, but knew that her daughter had indeed learned to "trust in God."

It had been decided between Mr. Saunders and his friends that Abbie had better go to the village and remain until the suit was finished. His friends urged this because she would be safer, and they would be free to go or come as they chose. To this she agreed, and two or three staunch friends promised to meet at Mr. Saunders' about midnight that night to accompany the father and daughter to the village.

Preparation was made for the journey, and at the appointed hour their friends arrived. Their hearts were filled with pity as they looked upon the bereaved family, as they, with tear-stained faces, gathered around Abbie. She was pale, but calm and firm, as she bade them good-by and entered the sleigh.

The father followed with tottering step. One of his friends remonstrated, entreating him to stay at home, and promising to guard Abbie with his life, to which entreaty the others added their voices.

"No, no," said the old man, shaking his head in a determined way; "I must see her safely housed, and among staunch friends, or I cannot rest."

They said no more, and drove away in silence, but the scene thus inscribed upon their memory would never be forgotten. They had known and respected Mr. Saunders since his entrance into the neighborhood. They well remembered the day when Abbie entered the church, attired as a bride, and leaning on the arm of her young husband. They had looked upon it as an ill-assorted match at the time, for, though they knew no ill of the young man, yet he was not a universal favorite. Mr.

White, one of the men who now attended Abbie, had remarked upon the wedding day that, in his opinion, it would not take much to make Rushford a villain. They had heard of the treatment his young wife had received at his hands, and now he had demonstrated the cruelty of his heart by not only robbing her of her child, but needlessly exposing its life by not using precautions that lay in his power to protect its tender form from the biting winds of a Minnesota winter. And the mother was obliged to fly, under the cover of the night, to escape further violence.

On reaching town, after a dreary ride of six miles, they received admittance into the house of a friend, but, as his house stood upon the outskirts of the town, it was not considered a safe place, and another was procured in the heart of the town, where she was surrounded by friends. Here her father left her and returned home.

Abbie scarcely expected that her babe would be brought in by those who had gone in pursuit, but hour after hour passed, and no tidings came of either pursuer or pursued.

At last, about two o'clock, a man rode into town upon a jaded horse, and was immediately recognized as one of the pursuing party. He was at once surrounded by an eager crowd, who clamored for the news. Jim Brooks, as the man was called, dismounted from his horse and was led away to shelter and food, as he had declared he would tell nothing until he had some "grub," as he had eaten nothing since evening.

While he is thus occupied, we will go back and follow the brothers in their flight.

CHAPTER XIX.

THEY stood so much in fear of pursuit that they did not slacken their speed until they were several miles from the scene of their exploit, and even then they did not stop altogether.

On entering the sleigh, the babe, who had been awakened by the rough handling and the piercing wind, began to scream at the top of its voice, utterly refusing to be comforted by the means its inhuman father had provided. In vain he tried to still its cries. It would not heed his efforts, but continued to cry, until, tired and weary, it fell into a deep sleep. This was a great relief to the brothers. They had been afraid that its cries would attract the attention of some passers-by. To guard against this they had taken an unfrequented road through a sparsely-settled country, and had completely enveloped the father in the blankets, thus inducing any passer-by to believe the child was with its mother.

This to Steve was a very unpleasant position. To be enveloped, head and ears, in blankets, with a crying child, did not quite meet his ideas of comfort, and more than once he regretted the course he

(234)

had taken, and was almost persuaded to take it back. But, having but little love for the child, and no conception of the danger of its position, he would not yield to this desire, but determined to carry out his threat, even if he was obliged to be nurse the whole distance home. When, therefore, his brother advised the return of the child, he flatly refused.

It was not his intention to leave the neighborhood without another attempt to secure Abbie, so, after going some distance, they took a roundabout way and returned to within six miles of Mr. Saunders' residence, where, finding a small house standing in an isolated position and inhabited by an old Dutchman and his wife and two small children, they decided to apply for shelter.

The babe had awakened, and was crying in a weak, faint voice. The Dutchman's wife, upon hearing the child, immediately gave her consent, but what was her surprise, when the blankets were thrown back, to see, not a woman, as she had expected, but a man emerge from the sleigh with the child in his arms, and enter the house. Seating himself by the fire, he proceeded to unwrap the heavy blankets in which the child was enveloped. Recovering from her surprise, she, in a slightly broken accent, inquired for the mother.

Steve had not forgotten his acting, and his tongue was as ready as ever. Pretending to wipe a tear from his eyes, which he took care not to raise to the woman's face, he said in trembling tones that the poor little thing's mother was very sick; that the babe had also been sick, and that, as proper help could not be procured, and as both were likely to die, he had been advised to take the child to his mother, who lived some twelve miles further on. He had hoped to reach there that night, but as it was so late, and the babe seemed so weak, he dared go no farther.

All the mother feeling was aroused in the woman. She took little Ella tenderly in her arms, and, sitting down by the fire, proceeded, as only a mother knows how, to relieve the wants of the little one. It was indeed in a pitiable plight. Stripping off its garments, and bathing the little form in a gentle, loving manner, she dressed it in some cast-off clothing that had once been worn by her own sturdy boys. She then tried to feed it some warm milk, but it would take but little, and seemed to be in a stupor, from which it could not be aroused. After doing all she could for its comfort, she made a bed of pillows, and, placing it near the fire, laid the little form gently down, and began active preparations for supper for the two men who were sitting by the fire.

They had eaten nothing since morning, and when they were invited to partake of the humble fare, they soon made way with the food prepared.

Mrs. Thaylor had not taken much notice of her older guests, having her attention so thoroughly taken up with the little one, but now, as she sat op-

posite the father while he ate, and studied his countenance, a feeling of distrust which she could not
shake off or account for stole over her.

Mr. Thaylor said but little, but watched the two
men furtively. He was out with Bill when Steve
told his artful story, which had not been questioned
by Mrs. Thaylor, but had received an explanation
of their strange appearance from Bill, who, not being an adept at deceit, had told such a disconnected
story that his host's suspicions were aroused at
once. Feeling sure there was some foul play, he
watched them narrowly, and after they had resumed
their seat by the fire, attempted to draw them out,
in which he did not succeed.

Being weary, they soon requested permission to
retire. When they were alone, they compared notes,
and as soon as Bill had given an account of his
talk with Thaylor, they saw that they were in a fair
way for a muss. However, thinking they would
be a match for the Dutchman and his wife, they dismissed their fears, and were soon sound asleep, and
did not wake until morning.

After the supper things had been put away, Mrs.
Thaylor took the little one in her arms once more,
and, gazing tenderly into its tiny face while she held
the little cold feet to the fire (they had so far re-
sisted all attempts to warm them), she told her husband the touching story that had been told to her.

He listened attentively, then asked, "He said the
mother was sick, did he?"

"Yes," said his wife, "so sick they don't think she will live. Poor little lamb!" kissing the child.

"Well, the other told me she was dead."

"Dead! Land-a-massy, is it possible she is dead, and the poor father does not know it! What will he do? He shed tears like a child when he came in."

"Humph!" said Thaylor, moving uneasily in his chair, and watching his wife as she lovingly caressed the little one.

"Poor, dear little lamb!" she murmured. "How sick it is! It does not notice anything. But there, I must lay the poor thing down, for I must wash and dry its clothes against they start in the morning."

Laying the babe gently on its little bed, she took the kettle that was singing by the fire, and, pouring some water into a tub, set to work with a will. She soon had the clothes sweet and clean. Then, hanging them by the fire to dry, and clearing away the washing utensils, she once more sat down and took the child in her arms.

It was now nearly ten o'clock. The babe had scarcely stirred since she laid it down. Mr. Thaylor sat moodily watching the coals, a look of perplexity settling upon his countenance. As Mrs. Thaylor took the babe in her arms, a faint moan escaped its lips, followed by a rattling sound in its throat, and hard breathing. They looked at each other in alarm. The woman turned her head to listen, as if

to ascertain if the two men in the loft were awake.
But the heavy stentorian breathing soon indicated
that they were both sleeping soundly. She cast an
inquiring look at her husband, but he shook his
head, saying, "No, do not disturb them." Then,
moving his chair nearer hers, they eagerly scanned
the face of the little sufferer.

It bore the marks of great suffering, but it was
by no means as thin as might have been expected
from a long spell of sickness and neglect. Its cheeks
were round and plump, and its arms and hands
wrinkled with fat, and felt plump as Mrs. Thaylor
took them in her own. Noticing this, the husband
reached forward and took the little hand in his, then,
looking in his wife's face, he said in a low voice, so
as to escape the ears of the sleepers :—

"This child hasn't been sick long. Those cheeks
and arms show that it has not only been well, but
has had the best of care."

"But it is surely sick now," said the woman,
startled by the look of her husband.

"Yes, but it is from the exposure of to-day.
Depend upon it, the child has been stolen."

"Oh, land-a-massa!" cried the terrified wife.
"Can it be so? Oh, whatever shall we do?"

"Be quiet, wife; you disturb the little one. See
how hard it breathes again. There, that is better,"
as the child again became quiet, and its breath
came more evenly. "Now do not disturb it again,
and I will tell you what I think."

In a low tone he told her that he believed that the man had a grudge against the father of the child, and had stolen it, and was carrying it off; that his story was a mere fabrication to deceive them, and that the sickness of the babe was caused by the exposure of the day.

"There," said he, "see that. That's just the way little Frankie acted after we had had him out on a cold day. The doctor said it was croup. Look! See that motion. See how hard it breathes."

The babe had become suddenly restless, throwing up its arms as if in pain, while its breath came short and quick. It languidly opened its large blue eyes and fixed them upon the woman's face in mute appeal, its nostrils dilated, its lips tightly drawn.

"Oh, land-a-massa!" cried the woman, "it will surely die. Call its father quick, and send him for the doctor. Oh, be quick!" she cried, as she saw his hesitation, forgetting in her fear for the babe her suspicions of a moment before. "Be quick, or it will be too late."

"No, no," said her husband in an excited tone. "It would now be too late. It is three miles to the doctor's, and it would be all over before he could go half the distance. We must do something ourselves if we hope to save its life. Do you not remember what the doctor did for Frankie? Here, give me the child while you work. Be still as death and do not awaken them. I cannot bear that they should approach the child."

He took the babe in his arms, when his wife placed a pillow so that the little form might lie more easily.

Filling a basin from the kettle, which she had re-filled and placed by the fire, she soon enveloped the little feet in cloths wrung from the warm water, then, placing the same the whole length of its body, she proceeded to envelop its throat in cloths, wet first in hot then in cold water, and was soon rewarded by seeing the patient somewhat relieved and breath·ing more easily. The nostrils resumed their natural motion; the drawn, painful expression left its mouth, and in half an hour it sank into a peaceful slumber, and they knew it was saved.

With a sigh of relief the wife looked into the face of her husband. The troubled expression had re-turned to his face, and he was looking steadily at the clothes of the child, as they hung by the fire. He rose and examined them closely. They were neatly made of fine material, deeply embroidered, evidently by the mother's own hand.

Turning to his wife, he said, "I am sure that this man has no right to the child, and it shall not leave this house until I know more about it."

"But how will you prevent it?" asked the wife, in evident alarm. "They are two heavy, powerful men, and if your suspicions are true, they must be very bad."

"I have thought of that," replied he. "We will send Johnny over to Parkers' as soon as it is light,

16 •

and ask him and his two sons to come over as soon
as they can. We'll keep the men till they come,
then we'll be able to do whatever is necessary to
keep the child."

They watched by the side of the little one all
night. At the first streak of day little Johnny was
on his way to Parker's. At length, hearing the
men stirring upstairs, Mrs. Thaylor rose and set
about preparing breakfast, but she worked as slowly
as possible, in order to delay the scene that must
surely come, and give their friends time to arrive.
As the father sat by the fire, impatiently waiting the
progress of the meal, she decided to try to obtain
peaceable possession of the child, and, telling him of
its narrow escape the night before, she begged him
to allow it to remain in her care until it should entirely recover, promising, as soon as it was safe, to
take the child to its mother. This he refused, and
seemed very uneasy and anxious to be on his way.

At length the two men were seated at the breakfast table. As the woman took the babe in her
arms and began to feed it some warm milk, the
father angrily ordered her to dress the child in its
own clothes, as he must be off as soon as possible.
The woman refused to obey him, declaring that
the child was not able to be dressed, and must not
be taken out that day.

Steve had risen from the table, and replied angrily
that he had only asked her to take care of the child
for the night, that he was willing to pay her any

price for her trouble, but that the child was going with him. If she did not dress it, he would take it as it was. He was angry at the manner in which Thaylor regarded him, and was working himself into a towering passion. He told them it was none of their business who the child belonged to, how he came by it, or what he did with it; that he believed that the story that the child was sick had only been concocted by them to frighten him, but they would find that he was not to be frightened, and the child he would have at any cost.

Suddenly the burly form of Baker entered the room, followed by his two stalwart sons. Steve's countenance quickly fell. The three men were well armed, for Johnny had told his story well, and as he brought up the rear he stepped to his father's side, and looked the angry man full in the face.

Steve saw at a glance that he was trapped. Not a word was spoken. He stalked silently out of the room, followed by Bill. As soon as they had gained a sufficient distance so as not to be overheard, but near enough to watch the door of the house, they paused and held a consultation.

Meanwhile Thaylor eagerly related to his friends what we have already told. They readily agreed that his suspicions were well-grounded, and volunteered their assistance. Just then the two men walked toward the house.

Steve's face wore a smile of exultation. Bowing to them in mock politeness, he said: "No doubt, gentlemen, you think yourselves right in upholding this woman in her refusal to give me my child. It does indeed seem strange that I should be traveling alone with so young a child, but, as I said before, I am the father of the child. I intended to take it back to its mother, as the thought of returning without it, and the grief of its mother when she should discover that I had left it, was too much for me to bear. This I did not feel bound to explain to you, supposing it to be my own business. When the woman refused to give up the child, I grew angry. For this I crave pardon, but request that the child be immediately prepared for its journey, as I am anxious lest my wife, becoming conscious, should discover the absence of the child, and thus suffer needless pain."

He paused, but, as the woman still hesitated, he continued: "If you still doubt my word, I will agree that you and your husband shall accompany the child and see it safe in its mother's arms. That is certainly as fair a proposal as you could ask."

After some consultation they agreed to his terms, and, making as speedy preparations as possible, they set out, Barker kindly taking their little ones home with him until their return.

Mrs. Thaylor had made the child as comfortable as possible in some of her babe's cast-off wraps, and, with a large bottle of nicely-prepared milk, hoped to find no trouble in keeping it so to the end of her journey.

After driving some three miles over the bleak prairie, they entered a deep ravine, where they were completely hidden from view. Here they came to a sudden halt, and Bill, taking a sled stake in one hand, held the lines with the other. Steve caught up an ax, which had lain hidden in the straw with which the bottom of the sleigh was covered, and, springing out, advanced to the side of the sleigh.

Mr. and Mrs. Thaylor were comfortably seated, while Mrs. Thaylor held the babe in her arms. He commanded them, in no gentle tone, to lay down the child and dismount, as he had no further need of their assistance. The astonished pair instantly saw that they were beaten, and as there was no use of resisting the command, they at once rose and alighted.

By the time they were fairly out, Steve had sprung into the sleigh, Bill whipped up his horses, and the crestfallen pair were left standing in the snow, which was nearly a foot deep, with no alternative but to walk back that long three miles across the prairie, while the babe they had striven so hard to protect was again in the hands of its captors. As soon as Steve regained the sleigh, he caught the child from where it lay, and, holding it far above his head, he danced and shouted at the pair whom he had so cleverly outwitted more like a savage than a civilized man.

They soon disappeared, however, and the pair turned slowly toward home. But you may be sure they did not soon forget their adventure, and when, twelve years after, having learned the facts in the case, they visited the mother and daughter in their home not twelve miles from the spot where they were left in the snow, their story had lost nothing either in interest or length.

Steve and Bill, after leaving the Dutchman and his wife to find their way back as best they could, continued to drive swiftly forward until they were not far from Mr. Saunders' place, when they halted in a small grove and again held a consultation. Bill was for leaving the babe at Mr. Saunders, and then leaving the country. To this Steve would only agree on conditions, and they were that if Abbie came herself for the child she should have it, but he would not give it to any of the "Saunders clique." Bill finally agreed, and they drove forward.

They soon reached the gate. Mrs. Saunders ran eagerly to the door, hoping to get the child. Steve called for Abbie, saying she could have her babe if she cared enough for it to come to the sleigh after it, if not, he would not give her another chance.

Mrs. Saunders replied that Abbie was not there, but that she would see that she had the babe before night, if he would give it to her, in her anxiety coming close to his side.

He took care that she should see the child, but utterly refused to either give it up or to believe that Abbie was not there, using all his arts to entice

Alice Morton

"HE AGAIN HELD THE BABE FAR ABOVE HIS HEAD."

her to come out. He made solemn promises not to molest her if she came, while he fully intended to entice her to his side, then force her into the sleigh and drive away before anyone could interfere.

Becoming convinced that further parley was useless, he told Bill to drive on, telling Mrs. Saunders, who had pleaded in vain for the child, that Abbie had lost her last chance of getting her babe. Then, springing to his feet, he again held the babe far above his head, while he performed the same gyrations as before.

Arriving at old Mr. Thomas', the same scene was enacted, the women trying in vain to get possession of the babe, when its little form was again held aloft, while its inhuman father danced and shouted like a madman. The cries of the child were distinctly heard until lost in the distance.

They had chosen the best time possible for this exhibition, as none but women were at home in either house. Raz and several others had searched all day and far into the night for the abductors, but for some unaccountable reason had not discovered their track since losing it soon after starting. After taking some refreshment and resting a few hours, they had again started out, just at break of day, and were still absent. Anda and old Mr. Thomas had gone to the village. So it happened that when most needed they were absent, and the brothers went on their way rejoicing.

After leaving Mr. Thomas' they were obliged to

make a short circuit in order to avoid the village. Then they took a direct route for home, never stopping until compelled by hunger and fatigue to seek shelter for the night. Taking warning by their first blunder, they this time agreed upon what story they should tell to account for the possession of the child. This was that, the mother being dead, they were, at the earnest request of the mother before her death, taking the child to its grandparents in Wisconsin, and that the mother had died at the house of a brother who had refused to give up the child, and had threatened to recover it before they left the State. Fearing he might attempt to carry his threat into execution, they entreated the lady who took care of the child to inform them immediately if anyone should call during the night. They again retired to an upper room, leaving the babe in the hands of strangers.

But there was little danger that it would be neglected, and again was Abbie's babe faithfully watched and carefully nursed the livelong night, while far away her arms and heart were aching for the privilege.

But we must return to the village, where we left Jim Brooks making way with the ham, eggs, and other eatables placed before him, while a crowd stood near the door, anxiously waiting his appearance and the story he was to tell.

CHAPTER XX.

T last, unable to eat another morsel, he entered the barroom and signaled to them that the story was about to begin.

"You see," said he, " me and a lot of others joined Raz with the determination of hunting the rascals down. We hadn't gone far, however, when we completely lost their track, and do all we could, we could not strike it again. They had taken a different course from what they should to get to Wisconsin, so we made up our minds we'd find 'em hid somewhere not far off. But I'll be plagued if we could find hide or hair of 'em, and it was after midnight before we got there to Saunders' Raz was mighty oneasy to get home, for fear there would be trouble before we got there, but when he found that his sister had been sent down here, he felt better. He says all they took the young-un for was to get hold of her.

"Well, then, after getting a bite to eat, and resting awhile, we put out again, just as it was coming light. But, do all we could, we could get no clue till about ten or eleven o'clock, when we came upon their track about three miles from here, going towards Saunders. We were mighty glad on't, for

(249)

we had about gi'n up beat. We followed on as fast
as we could, and reached Saunders' about half past
'leven. We found that they had been there with the
young-un, but refused to give it to anyone but the
mother. She wasn't at home, and he drove off
holding the babe above his head and dancing and
shouting like mad. The cowardly villain! if we
could have caught him, he would have danced a
different jig before now. Well, when the boys heard
this, they dashed after them as fast as their tired
horses could go, never asking how long they had
been gone, or nothing, bent on catching them at last.
When we got to old Thomas', we found they had
been there too, going through the same performance
as before. Young Mrs. Saunders says the babe was
crying, so they know they were not fooled. We
asked how long they had been gone and found that
they were at least two hours ahead of us, so we concluded to go home and get fresh horses and start
again. Raz declares that he won't sleep until the
rascals are caught, and several of the boys say they
will stand by him. They sent me on to see which
way they went, and then come here. They have
taken the old road through the woods and gone
straight for Wisconsin. Raz wanted me to tell you
boys that if any of you was ready to lend a helping
hand, you are to meet him at the bridge at three."

It was now two o'clock, but at the stroke of three
a band of mounted men were at the appointed spot.
On counting up their men there was found to be

twenty-three. They at once decided that so large
a number was not necessary, and all but ten returned
to the village. The rest pressed on eagerly after
the brothers.

While daylight lasted it was easy to track them,
but as the darkness increased the difficulties became
greater. They might have stopped at one of the
many farmhouses along the road, and it was more
than likely their pursuers would pass without suspecting the fact. As the snow began to fall, de-
stroying all hope of tracking their enemy, the pursuers halted and held a council.

Some were of the opinion that they had already
passed them, and all agreed that further pursuit was
useless. They turned their horses' heads reluctantly
toward home, where in due time they arrived, mad-
der if not wiser men. And their feelings were in
no wise soothed when, a few days later, they learned
that they had turned back just three miles short of
the house where their intended victims were then
sleeping, oblivious of danger, and from which they
continued their journey, bearing with them the
almost inanimate form of the little Ella.

Although, through the kind and judicious treatment of Mr. and Mrs. Thaylor, she had escaped that
terrible scourge to children, the croup, yet her little
form could not bear up against the exposure she
was obliged to endure, and when at last she was
placed in the hands of Mrs. Harrison, she was more
dead than alive, and but little hopes were enter-
tained that she would live until morning.

Shocked and surprised at the condition of the babe, and at the nonappearance of the mother, as soon as the children had retired and they were left alone with their brother, Mr. and Mrs. Harrison demanded an explanation of the strange affair.

Steve, since eating his supper, had sat near his babe, sometimes gazing at its waxen face, in which no signs of consciousness, and we might almost add of life, appeared, or, covering his face with his hands, strove to shut out from his mind the terrible consequences of his rash act, which now, in his cooler moments, stood forth in all its hideousness. He remembered his inhuman exultation when the plan was proposed to him, and his untiring efforts to carry it out, how he had deceived his brother in regard to Abbie's readiness to leave her friends, and had misconstrued her actions lest he should be undeceived. He thought of the yearning, pleading look in the face of the young mother as she begged for the restoration of her child, of the anger he had felt at her firmness in regard to her own position, and of his unspoken threat against the life of the child for which she pleaded.

He shuddered as he thought of this, for he knew that in his heart he had longed for the courage to do the deed, and thus trample her heart beneath his feet. He thought of his cruel exposure of the little one, who now lay so calm and pale before him, slowly breathing its life away. His very soul shrank with horror at the terrible picture. His babe, his pure, innocent babe, dying, and by his hand!

Until arriving here he had quieted his mind with the thought that when he should place the babe in the care of his sister, it would revive; but he could no longer doubt its true condition, and he well knew that should the babe die now, he was as surely its murderer as though he had put his dia-bolical threat into execution. The thought was .torture, and as he gazed on the waxen face, he deeply regretted the course he had taken.

When, therefore, he was requested to give an account of his strange act, he almost decided to tell the whole truth. But ere he could frame words with which to speak, his evil nature gained control, and, arguing that it could in no way benefit the injured parties, and would bring reproach from his friends, he again had recourse to equivocation and falsehood.

Trusting to his ready tongue, he began his story, but such was the state of his mind that, though he sought as far as possible to shield himself from blame and implicate Abbie, his story was so discon-nected and improbable that both were convinced that he was hiding the truth. Their hearts were filled with indignation, not only because he could be capable of such meanness, but that he could, in the presence of his dying child, attempt to shield himself with falsehood. From his own showing they felt fully convinced that his young wife had been cruelly treated, and that the abduction of the child had been actuated more by revenge against the

mother than love for the child. Indeed, had he
loved the babe he would rather have borne the
separation than thus subject the little one to exposure which could scarce fail to result in its death.

But they were too anxious about the fate of the
babe to wish to reproach the father.   For two long
days and nights the babe seemed to flutter between
life and death.   At last, to the unspeakable relief of
all, it showed signs of recovery.   When it was pronounced out of danger, Steve's friends all joined
in an attempt to persuade him to return it to its
mother.

This he refused to do, for, as the fear of its death
vanished, his anger returned in all its force.   But
finally, after the lapse of three weeks, yielding to
the entreaty of his friends and his own curiosity,
he again bent his steps toward Minnesota, where we
will leave him and return to Abbie.

In blissful ignorance of the condition of her child,
and having full faith in God that he could and would,
even though it should be at the eleventh hour,
again allow her to press her babe to her breast (for
so plain had come to her, as she knelt in her chamber that day, the full assurance that her prayer had
been heard and would be answered, that she had
not for a moment doubted), she had so resolutely
held her emotions in check that, but for her pale
face, from which the color had entirely disappeared,
the pained expression of the mouth, and the unwonted fire in her eyes, her friends might have been

deceived into the belief that she felt no interest in the fate of her child.

Though she seemed so calm, and her faith in God's promise was so strong, yet she could not shut her eyes to the fact that her darling must suffer the penalty of outraged nature, and, though it should be again restored to her, its frail form be doomed to untold suffering, from which she was powerless to relieve it. Horrible pictures of suffering and neglect tortured her brain, struggle as she would to drive them out, and but for the continued prayer that rose from her heart, "O God, help thy servant to trust in thee!" she must have sunk under their weight. But ever and anon as the cry rose to heaven, the answer seemed borne back to her, "Trust thou in me, for I will surely deliver thee from thy affliction."

Let those who will scoff at prayer. Abbie would not have exchanged her faith in prayer and her trust in God for all the wealth the world could give.

Mr. Sherman, the gentleman into whose family she had been welcomed, was a minister, the same who had performed her marriage ceremony. His wife also was a pious woman. They sympathized deeply with her in her affliction, heaping many kindnesses upon her, and trying as far as they were able to lighten her grief.

A room was provided for her near their own, and every comfort furnished. But solitude is a poor antidote for a diseased mind. It often became intol-

erable to her, and she would join the family in the
large sitting room. Here was life and bustle enough,
but she was still doomed to inactivity. Mrs. Sherman thought that in supplying every known want,
while she scarcely allowed her to wait upon herself,
she was doing all that could be done to lighten the
burden poor Abbie had to bear. But to Abbie,
who had always been accustomed to active labor,
this idle life was almost unbearable, and she often
begged to be allowed to assist in the household
labor, but was as often refused. Mrs. Sherman,
knowing nothing of Abbie's feelings, feared that it
would be taking advantage of her position, while
Abbie, being young and sensitive, and fearing that
she might not give satisfaction, dared not urge the
matter.

Thus day after day went by with nothing to relieve
their monotony, while Mr. Sherman, who was reading the history of Flavius Josephus, would take his
seat by the fire and read aloud, sometimes for hours,
in that slow, monotonous tone so peculiar to him,
emphasizing each word as though the whole sense of
the book depended upon it, until Abbie grew almost
wild. Though Mr. Sherman was a fair speaker,
he was by no means a pleasant reader, and Abbie
acquired such an antipathy to that book that she
could never after listen to the reading of it with any
degree of patience.

As soon as it was ascertained that the brothers
were indeed gone, Abbie's counsel had taken steps

by which they might be informed of their arrival at
B. By this means she had learned of the safety
of her child, that it was in good hands, that its
arrival had created a strong prejudice among
Steve's relatives against him, that they were unani-
mous in urging him to return it to its mother, and
that they had taken steps to guard against its removal
from its present position without their immediate
knowledge.

This was a great consolation to her. She had
great confidence in the integrity of his people,
especially this sister in whose care the child had
been placed. Feeling thankful for the consolation
thus unexpectedly vouchsafed to her in her affliction,
she strove more earnestly to endure her grief quietly,
if not cheerfully.

After remaining a week at the house of the minister she one day received a call from the wife of
the village merchant, Mrs. Anthony, who, having
heard from Mrs. Sherman that Abbie seemed to
desire employment, and being in need of assistance,
called to secure her services. Her proposal was
gladly accepted by our heroine, for she was by no
means averse to labor. She was soon established
in her new position, and entered with hearty good
will into the performance of her duties, where, by
her ready hands, her quiet manner, and her strict
attention to duty, she soon won the respect of Mrs.
Anthony, who often tried to win from her a promise
to make her house home in the future.

17

But though she was as happy as possible with her new friends, she did not forget her absent one, or cease to pray for its return. Her faith was strong, yet her heart seemed at times almost to burst with her intense desire to clasp her darling to her breast, and she wildly longed to fly away on the wings of the wind to the side of her precious one. But no; she must wait—wait. What a terrible meaning the words had to the stricken woman! When would her waiting be over, and her babe safe in her arms again?

Flying to her room, and falling on her knees, there would rise to heaven such an earnest prayer as seldom comes from the lips of one so young. Then, as if straight from the lips of the Mighty One, would come the words: "Trust in me, my child, for I will never leave thee nor forsake thee." She would then return to her duty with that smile of true happiness which only faith can give.

Three weeks had passed thus pleasantly away, when one morning Mr. and Mrs. Anthony set out for a small town some twenty miles away, where they were to spend the night at the house of a brother, and return the next day, leaving Abbie to care for the house during their absence, with Irvin and Josie, their only children, aged respectively fifteen and thirteen, for company.

The children were soon off to school, and Abbie was alone in the house for the first time since entering it. A feeling of utter loneliness took possession of her, and it was some time before she could shake it off. But she went resolutely to work, and had soon nearly forgotten her fears.

Suddenly there was a step at the door. She started and turned pale. Then, thinking her fears were foolish, she stepped forward and opened the door. There upon the step stood the man of all others that she most dreaded to see, Steve Rushford.

He was dressed in faultless taste, and held in his hand a new volume, evidently just purchased, between the leaves of which one finger was placed as though he had just been reading, while on his face played that sanctified smile which Abbie had such good cause to remember, and which he was never known to wear except when bent on some rascality.

Abbie stood for a moment perfectly paralyzed with fear, before she attempted to close the door, which he prevented by placing one foot in the way.

"Oh, don't be in a hurry!" he said, in his most persuasive tone. "I wish to speak with you."

"But I do not wish to speak with you," she replied, again trying to shut the door.

But he was not to be balked in this way, and, pushing open the door, he entered the room and closed the door after him.

Then he said: "You need not be afraid. I only wish to speak with you, and give you this; and he held out the book which he had in his hand, and which Abbie instantly recognized as the Bible.

Her thoughts instantly reverted to the last week of her stay with him. In his efforts to draw some word of complaint from her, he had taken the babe to the fire, and then, taking from a shelf a Bible that had been a gift from her brother, proceeded to read aloud to the child for some time.

Then, turning to her, he said, "Why, Abbie, this child is a perfect heathen. She don't show a bit of reverence for the Bible."

Again turning to the babe, he gave it quite a lecture on the sacredness of the Bible, quite enough, Abbie thought, to prove that he at least had no reverence for it. Then, as if struck with a sudden thought, he added, "Oh, I know what I can do! If I cannot make her learn the Bible, I can at least make her eat it."

Suiting the action to the word, he tore leaf after leaf from the book and stuffed them into the mouth of the helpless child, until it was nearly suffocated, resisting so long the efforts of the mother to take the child that it was with difficulty she could bring back its breath. At last the scraps of paper were removed and the child breathed freely once more, but so great had been the fright of the mother that she burst into tears, when he said, sneeringly: "There, don't cry. I am sorry I tore your book, but the babe needed it, and I'll buy you another some day."

As soon, therefore, as Abbie recognized the book, this incident came fresh to her mind, and as he held

the book toward her, she felt such indignation at
his heartless cruelty and bold effrontery that for
once she longed for the strength to strike him to
the ground.

He continued to hold out the book, till, gaining
control of her voice, she said, " I do not want your
book."

"What, don't want a Bible? How wicked you
must be! Well," opening it, and taking from between its leaves a lock of shining baby hair, while
his face lit up with a cruel smile, " here is something
I think you will want. See, I have brought you a
lock of your baby's hair."

She turned deadly pale, and shrank back as
though she had received a blow.

He advanced toward her, still holding the shining curl in his hand. "I should think you would
want this to remember your baby by."

"O God!" she thought, as she recoiled still farther, unable to speak, "can it be he fears I shall forget my babe? No, no, it is only a new device to
torture me."

Sending up a prayer to heaven for strength, she
arose and stood before him, pale but defiant. "Sir,
I will not touch your cruel memento, and I request
you to leave the house immediately."

"What," said he, not heeding her last words,
"not accept a lock of your baby's hair, when it is so
far away, and you may never see it again? So! you
must be heartless as well as wicked."

He paused to watch the effect of his words, then
continued, after looking her over as if she were
some strange animal:—

"A cruel, heartless mother! After her babe has
been taken away, and she has not seen it for so
long, she will not take a lock of its hair. Mon-
strous!"

These words, and many more of like import, were
uttered by him as he stood with his back against
the door, thus, as he thought, effectually hindering
the escape of his victim. They were uttered in
slow, murmuring tones, as if speaking to himself,
while every word entered the mother's heart like a
knife.

At last she could endure it no longer, and, throwing up her arms in agony, she cried out, "Oh, leave
me, leave me, I beg!"

Her answer was a derisive laugh.

Starting to her feet, she cried, "Leave this house
instantly, or I will leave it," and she laid her hand
on the door leading through the hall and out at a
door in the front part of the house. This door was
seldom used, as the undisturbed snow on its step
had told Steve before he entered. Abbie did not
remember that it had been opened since her arrival,
so, although she had thought of that way of escape,
she dared not attempt it for fear of becoming a prisoner in the hall, until driven to it by very desperation.

Steve, seeing her look of determination, and not

caring to draw the attention of the villagers, as she probably would if she left the house, very willingly signified his intention of going, only waiting long enough to hope he might see her again soon, as he had important business to transact with her.

The house in which she was stood at some distance from any other, and, not daring to remain longer alone, she hurriedly threw on her wraps, and, securing the door behind her, went quickly down the street and entered the house of a Mr. Walters. She had scarcely entered the house when she received a message from Steve, delivered in the hearing of the inmates of the house, saying that he wished to see her and make some necessary arrangements, as he had decided to bring back the child if such was her request.

On leaving the house in which he had so cruelly treated Abbie, he had immediately entered the village store, where several men were lounging, and hurriedly said that he had come to make arrangements for returning the child to its mother, and that he had visited the house where she resided but had been refused admittance.

"Where is the child?" asked one of the loungers.

"It is not far off," replied Steve readily, "and all I want is to make a reasonable bargain about the bringing up, and she shall have it."

"That's fair," said the man who had before spoken. "I guess I know what's the matter. The folks are all gone, and she was afraid."

Steve feigned great surprise at this information, and, after a moment's thoughtful silence, said, "Maybe you are right." Then, looking anxiously into the man's face, he continued: "Do you think she would come down here? She could not be afraid while you are all here. I did a foolish trick to take the babe in the first place. All my folks are down on me, and I don't like to take it back. But I don't want to give it to her without a word."

"That's fair," said the man again; "and if you say so, I'll go and ask her myself."

Steve seemed very grateful for the offer, and the self-appointed messenger started on his way, supposing the babe to be in the village, or at least in the immediate neighborhood. Seeing Abbie enter the house of Mr. Walters, he quickly followed and delivered his message with great gusto. He was greatly surprised to see on the mother's face, instead of the joy he expected, a look of annoyance and anger. She did not speak, and all looked at her in wonder and surprise.

It would not have been possible for her to explain her feelings at that moment. She did not believe that her child was near, or that he had any notion of returning it, and, still smarting under the cruel treatment she had but that hour received at his hands, is it strange that she did not receive the message with favor?

"Will you come?" again asked the messenger.

"No," was all the answer she gave, and it seemed

to her that she could not have uttered another word for her life.

"No!" echoed all three in a breath. "Why, woman, you surely are crazy!"

This was too much, and, burying her face in her hands, she wept as though her heart would break.

All were touched by her grief, and the woman quickly said: "Poor thing! you frighten her. Of course she does not want to go down there among a lot of men. Go and tell him to come here if he wants to see her."

"That's what's the matter," exclaimed Mr. Walters, evidently considering his wife a very smart woman.

"Are you willing?" asked the messenger, looking at Abbie.

She silently gave her assent, for her heart was too full for words. She believed the interview would only result in torture to her.

Mistaking her emotions, and in total ignorance of her morning's adventure, Mrs. Walters answered for her, "Of course she is willing, so go along."

He needed no further bidding, and left the house, but soon returned with the man he was in search of.

Steve had started nervously on, hearing that Abbie was at a neighbor's. He did not wish the occurrence of the morning to be made public, and it did not take him long to reach the designated place. He anxiously scanned the faces of Mr. and Mrs. Walters as he entered the room, and was soon

conviced that they had heard nothing. Thus placed
at his ease, he at once opened negotiations by saying that he had acted in a very foolish way in taking the child from its mother, that he sincerely regretted the rash act, but that he had been actuated
by a feeling of anger toward the Saunders' family.
He had thought that he could not see his child
brought up there, and in a moment of anger had
taken it away. But he deeply loved and pitied his
wife, and, remembering that she was not to blame
for the wrongs her family had committed, he had
concluded to bring back the babe, and if she was
willing to make an agreement that would allow of
his seeing it, and knowing it was properly brought
up, he would gladly give it to her. During this little speech his air was that of a man who, in a sudden fit of anger, had committed a rash act for which
he was willing to make all the amends in his power.

We have said that he was a good actor, and so
well did he act his part that his hearers did not for
a moment doubt his sincerity, and when he laid
down his rule of agreement they were ready to
believe that it was all right.

Abbie at once saw her mistake in coming to the
house of a comparative stranger, when a few steps
further would have taken her among staunch friends,
who would have understood his wiles. She at once
determined to make no agreement whatever. She
had no faith in him, and would not trust him so
much as to place herself in any degree in his power.

Having made her decision, she became calm and apparently interested, while he laid down the rules by which she was to be governed when she should get the child.

Firstly, she was not to stay at her father's; secondly, she was not to stay in any home provided by Raz; thirdly, he was to see the babe as often and as much as he pleased; fourthly, he was to have the privilege of supporting the child and have a voice in its education. He furthermore added that, in case Abbie should find trouble in securing a home on account of her agreement with him, he would see that she was provided for, even if he had to pay her board himself.

As we said before, after Abbie's decision had been made, she became calm and collected, and as firstly, secondly, thirdly, and fourthly were laid down by him, she could not help longing to speak, as some queries were presented to her mind.

He had grown quite eloquent in his little speech.

When at last he paused for her opinion, she asked, rather than said, "So you wish me to agree not to live at father's?"

"I certainly do, as I do not want my child brought up there."

"Quite a reasonable request," said she, sarcastically. "Neither am I to look to Raz for a home, nor accept one if he should offer it?"

"No, indeed!" he said, trying to look indignant.

"Another very reasonable request. And I am to

let you see the child as much and whenever you please?"

"Yes," with rather a crestfallen air, for he began to see that she was quizzing him.

"Now, let me see if I understand it aright. I am not to accept either of the homes that are likely to be offered me; I am to let you see Ella when and as long as you please; I am to accept of your support for her, and allow your control of her; and I, in case I cannot find a home, am to accept of one at your hands. It seems to me that I must either decline your generous offer, or that I had better go with you at once. And, as I am not prepared for that step, I must decline."

A smile had gradually gathered on the faces of the half dozen men who had assembled to witness the agreement, and, as she finished, it widened into a broad grin, or broke into a loud laugh.

Steve was fairly beaten, but, not wishing to acknowledge his defeat, he said: "I am sorry you do not at once accept my offer. I will give you till to-morrow at ten to make your final decision."

Without waiting for an answer, he left the house.

Abbie now desired to return home, but, fearful of further molestation, she hesitated.

"I would not go," said Mrs. Walters.

"But I must," replied Abbie. "Mrs. Anthony is not at home, and the house is alone. Yet I am afraid it is not safe."

"He surely would not molest you," said one.

"He surely would if he dare," she replied, and they were convinced that hers was no idle fear.

They immediately volunteered to keep close watch of him, and she returned home to take up her neglected duties.

CHAPTER XXI.

ON leaving Mr. Walters', Steve had immediately left town, and was not seen again that
day.

Rumors of the interview were rife in town. Some
extolled Abbie's courage and penetration, while
some thought that by her wit she had lost all chance
of getting the child, some doting mothers, in particular, saying they would have agreed to anything
until they got the child, then do as they pleased
about keeping their word.

But that was not her idea of right. Besides, she
had no faith that any agreement whatever would restore her babe, and if she did recover it, she did not
wish to be in any way beholden to him, but was determined to cut all acquaintance with him, if possible, for his actions that morning had convinced her
that his feelings were in no way changed or even
softened by what had passed.

Her troubles were the theme of the day throughout the town, and when Irvin returned from school
at night he was full of gallant determinations to protect Abbie from further molestation. But as they
sat around the fire after tea, he began to grow un-

(270)

easy, and made some excuse for leaving the house. Taking care that Abbie and his sister locked themselves in, he hurried away, and, finding some of his chums, soon had a band of gallant fellows ready to return with him and guard his charge during the night.

They crept noiselessly up to the house, lest Steve might be near. What was Abbie's surprise when she opened the door for Irvin, to see five stalwart boys follow him into the house! She was soon informed of their intentions, and, after thanking them, she set herself to work to entertain them, though, had she yielded to her own inclinations, she would have retired to her room.

Her efforts were seconded by Irvin and Josie, and they spent a very pleasant evening. No one to have seen them would for a moment have taken them for a besieged party.

At length, as the evening advanced, Abbie and Josie prepared to retire to their rooms. As Abbie was leaving the room, Irvin, who had not for a moment forgotten the purpose of the night, came to her and asked many questions in regard to the evil propensities of their common foe, whether he was a good shot, and whether he was "much on the climb," and understood opening of windows, all of which she answered as well as she could.

This was no easy task, as she felt that his questions were ludicrous in the extreme, and it was difficult to hide the smiles which both his words and his manner would naturally call forth. She succeeded in satisfying him, however, and passed on to her room, when the work of barricading the house began. Strange noises continued in every part of the house for a while, then all was still.

It will be remembered that the boys in the house were from fifteen to eighteen years old, and that the idea that the house might be attacked had not originated in their own brain. It had been talked of as probable by a knot of men in the hearing of young Anthony. All had been surprised at Steve's sudden disappearance after his talk with Abbie, and not a few were of the opinion that she might be made to suffer for thus boldly exposing him to ridicule. Though no one else considered it of enough importance to warrant any particular steps being taken, young Irvin, hearing their remarks, had formed his own opinion, the result of which we have seen.

Some of the boys had proposed to stay up all night, so as to hear the first approach of the enemy. But this idea was ruled down, as they would not like to sit up with neither fire nor light, and the presence of either would betray to the enemy that they were on their guard, and thus they might lose their fun after all. Numbers, coupled with locks, keys, and bolts, had made them bold, and they told one another that the one wish of their hearts was to meet the baby stealer face to face, though how they could hope to do this in their present position was hard to tell. They, therefore, decided to retire, but were fully determined not to close their eyes in sleep that night. But this resolution was soon forgotten, and all fell into a sound slumber, from which they did not awaken until morning.

At ten the next day Rushford again appeared, and sent a messenger to learn Abbie's decision. She gave the same answer she had given the day before. Not an hour had passed before she received another message, with which she refused to comply.

He was very angry at this continued refusal to parley with him, threatening to take the child away and never trouble her more, saying she never had had a mother's feeling, and but for pity for the babe she should never see it again.

In the meantime Mr. Anthony and wife returned, and she told them what had passed. After ascertaining her views in regard to the whereabouts of the babe, Mr. Anthony advised her not to answer any message from him unless delivered by or through her counsel, as they were no doubt on the alert, and if any good was to be gained they would not be slow to avail themselves of it. He commended her judgment in not meeting Steve, and then, leaving her with his wife, he repaired to the store, and took his place behind the counter, to the great relief of Irvin, who was thus set at liberty.

Irvin did not need long to decide what to do next. Leaving the store, he called Steve to one side and proceeded to make terms with him. He had been very angry on learning that Steve was

18

likely to be allowed to take the babe away again
(he did not doubt that it was concealed near by),
and was determined to prevent it if possible.

After a few moments' conversation he hastened
to the house. He felt sure of success, and, bursting
into the room where Abbie and his mother sat, he
proceeded, in a hurried way, to say that Abbie could
have her babe at last, that it was almost within her
grasp, and that she had only to come to his father's
store and talk a few words with Steve, when all
would be settled and the child restored to her.

At the first words Abbie, in spite of her former
experience, had started to her feet with hope bounding through every vein, but as he continued speaking, it died suddenly away, leaving her to sink into
a chair, pale and trembling. Oh, when would this
cruel torture cease, and she be allowed to rest?

Irvin stood by impatiently waiting for an answer,
when Mrs. Anthony asked what Steve wished to
talk about, and why the child was not brought along
if he was so anxious to give it up. He had been
hurt at the manner in which his message had been
received, and answered impatiently that he did not
know what Steve wished to talk about, but if Abbie
did not care enough for her babe to go to the store
for it, he had been deceived, and would do no more
about it.

"Be careful, my son," said Mrs. Anthony. "Remember you are speaking to a lady."

"Excuse me," said he apologetically. "I am disappointed. I have done all I can, and now, just as I am likely to succeed, she refuses even to come to the store and receive the child. It is too bad."

He seemed to think that all hope in the case must cease with his efforts, which had only failed through Abbie's refusal to co-operate with him. After using all his powers of persuasion on her, he left the house indignantly. Entering his father's store, where Steve stood waiting, he began hurriedly to announce his failure.

Mr. Anthony, surprised to see his son thus eagerly conversing with Rushford, inquired of what they were speaking. Irvin hesitatingly explained the matter to him. Mr. Anthony listened to all he had to say before quietly advising him to leave such matters for older heads hereafter. Then, turning to Rushford, he said: "It is impossible that you can understand in what a despicable light you appear before the people of this village. You have been about as mean as man can well be. If the babe is here, and you wish to return it, you had better do so immediately. If not, and you honestly wish to make any terms concerning it, you can go to Captain Johns or Squire Price, for Mrs. Rushford will receive no message except through them. The sooner matters are settled, the better," he added, as he retired to his place behind the counter.

Steve quickly left the store. His feelings were anything but enviable. He had observed several things during the last few days that had tended to

make him feel uneasy, and now the tone and manner of Mr. Anthony seemed to convey a covert
threat, and he began to see that the place was getting too warm for him. He knew nothing of the
pursuit of a few weeks before, for no one had been
on sufficiently good terms with him to tell him of it.
If he had known this, he might have been more
wary on his return. But as he had not then been
molested, he had felt quite secure. Now he thought
things looked a little squally, and he had better get
out of it as soon as he could. As he had no hopes
of any further concession on Abbie's part, he went
straight to Squire Price.

The hour that had passed since the entrance of
Irvin had been for Abbie the most wretched of all
that wretched month. She had thrown herself upon
the lounge, where she lay, pale and almost motionless, while visions of the past and future chased
one another through her throbbing brain, and her
heart seemed swollen almost to bursting. She did
not have power even to pray. All hope seemed to
have vanished from her forever.

She lay thus when the genial face of Squire Price
was seen as he entered the room, after a slight pre-
liminary tap at the door. At sight of him hope
once more revived, and she rose from her recum-
bent position, but she seemed to have lost the power
of speech. He broke the silence by saying that
he wished Abbie to come to his house to transact
some business.

"Is Steve there?" she asked eagerly.

"Yes," he said, "but you need not fear.   Indeed, I think you might better rejoice, for you are in a fair way to receive your child."

At this she sprang up eagerly, for she had faith in this man that he would not raise false hopes in her breast.   She was soon equipped, and they were in the street.

It was some distance to Squire Price's, and as they went along Abbie told him of her adventure of the day before.   He warmly commended her for her judicious course, and assured her that he believed Steve really intended to restore the child, but that he would no doubt have drawn her into some nefarious compact if possible.   She had been wise in not listening to him.

"But now I think it will be all right," he added, as they neared the house.

They entered the room and found Steve waiting. His exultant look was gone, and he seemed anxious. An agreement was soon made and signed, he agreeing to deliver the child to its mother in ten days, and she agreeing after receiving it to let him see it on reasonable occasions, she to be the judge as to what time was reasonable.   This agreement was to hold good till he on his part should sever it by taking undue advantage of it, when it should become null and void.

But when this was done, he still seemed in trouble, and at last said that he was not sure he could get the child, as he had made an agreement with Mr. Harrison by which he was not to have the child unless accompanied by the mother.

Here was a fresh blow to the poor mother's heart. We have seen in what a state of despondency Squire Price found her. From this state she had been roused by the hopeful words of her counsel, in whose judgment she had perfect confidence, and hope had risen to a high pitch, but as she heard these words it seemed felled by one terrible blow. She believed that he had been again playing with her.

But the Squire was not to be thus balked, and after a few moments' conversation he asked her to write a letter to Mr. Harrison, stating the case, to which he would sign his affidavit, and this he believed would do. Abbie eagerly seized the pen and wrote—she never afterward knew what. But it was considered sufficient, and, after writing his affidavit, and signing his name, Squire Price delivered it to Rushford, who immediately left the house and began his journey, anxious to put as many miles between him and the village as he could before night.

After receiving some good advice from Squire Price, Abbie returned to Mrs. Anthony, to pass those dreary ten days as best she might. She performed her duties as usual, but they did not awaken the same interest as before. She experienced a strange fluttering at her heart, a wild intermingling of hope and fear, which was fast wearing out her

constitution.   Her friends watched her with concern, and as the time drew near all felt that a disappointment would be fatal.

At length the appointed day arrived, and as the
hours passed slowly by and no tidings came, there
were many anxious faces in the little village.   Many
friends had gathered from the country round, anxious to hear the first news, and nothing was talked
of but the one all-important subject.

Abbie, pale and motionless, sat in her room at the
house of her kind friend and benefactress, Mrs. Anthony.   In this room there was a large window
that overlooked the town, and from it she could
watch the approach of anyone from Squire Price's.
By this window she sat, scarcely turning her eyes
from the street, yet never uttering a word.   About
three o'clock the long-looked-for messenger appeared in the person of the Squire, and it needed
but one look at his face, beaming with pleasure, to
tell her that the treaty had been successful, and that
the babe was safe.

We will not attempt to describe the scene that
followed.   Suffice it to say there was great rejoicing, and Abbie was conveyed to the home of the
Squire, almost without her knowledge.   So great
had been her anxiety that it seemed impossible to
believe that all was over, and her babe safe at last.

She was led into the room, and when she was
seated, the babe was placed in her arms.   She
gazed at the bundle as though she feared deception.

This was indeed the case. Poor heart! she had suffered so much that happiness seemed to have entirely lost its place in her heart, and when at last, after her long, weary waiting, the babe was on her knee, she dared not look into its face, lest she should find herself deceived.

Mr. Harrison had indeed refused to deliver the babe into the hands of its father, but had concluded to accompany him, bringing the babe along. He had taken such good care of it that it had hardly suffered at all from the journey, and he had that morning dressed it in the suit in which she had last seen it, and had not allowed its wraps removed till it should be placed in her arms, which act had been done by his own hands.

Now, seeing the mother's hesitation, he stepped forward and began to remove the clothing. She at first seemed willing, while an eager light shone in her eyes, but suddenly, as its face was about to be revealed, she pushed his hands away, and, clasping the bundle to her breast, she rocked to and fro, while low moans escaped her lips.

It was a heartrending scene, and not an eye in all that eager crowd remained dry.

Unable longer to endure the sight of so much joy, fear, and frenzy, the Squire motioned to Mr. Harrison, who stepped forward again, and gently but firmly removed the wraps. The mother had become passive, and gazed eagerly into the face of the infant, then minutely examined every article of

"SHE DARED NOT LOOK INTO ITS FACE LEST SHE FIND HERSELF DECEIVED."

dress. The babe, who had been sleeping till now, opened its blue eyes in wonder and fixed them on her face. She gazed into their blue depths a moment, then, with a glad cry, clasped the infant to her breast. All doubt of its identity was removed, and the scene that followed beggars description.

One by one the crowd dispersed, and she was left alone with her joy.

After some time she entered the family sitting room, where, besides the family, only Mr. Harrison and Rushford remained. Mr. Harrison had never seen her before that day, but as they conversed he grew more interested in her, and more dissatisfied with his brother-in-law. After half an hour's conversation he rose, and, bidding her good-by, left the house, followed by Steve, who did not seem anxious to prolong the interview.

His brow was black and stormy as he withdrew. But he was gone, and she was left with her friends, and, O joy! with her darling pressed to her breast. It seemed to her that she could never know sorrow again.

She returned to Mrs. Anthony that night. The next morning Mr. Harrison came to see her and if necessary render her some efficient aid. He talked very kindly to her, telling her that after all he had seen and heard he had no word of blame for her, and that he was glad it had fallen to his lot to care for her babe and restore it to her arms.

He told her that he had come prepared in his

own name and that of his wife to offer her a permanent home in his family. All had become strongly attached to the little Ella, and it was hard to give her up, but they felt that she had the first right, and one they were bound to recognize. He offered to bind himself by a written contract, which should be left in the hands of her counsel, to give her a home in his family as soon and as long as she pleased. She should fare in all things as well as they, and should always be respected as one of the family. He would also bind himself not to harbor or in any way encourage Steve while she should be there, or allow him to force himself into her presence, but would protect her from him at all times.

Abbie was deeply affected, the more so as by report she knew him to be an honorable and upright man, and one fully able to fulfill his word.

He offered to do this, and, leaving the paper in the hands of an attorney, to put it in her power to call upon him at any time to fulfill his word.

She felt truly grateful for his kindness, though she could not accept it, and, therefore, would not allow him to bind himself, and promised to consider him her friend, and should circumstances ever necessitate such a move, to consider his offer open to her.

Then he kissed the little Ella, and, bidding her an affectionate good-by, started for home alone, Steve refusing to go with him, saying he preferred to remain near his child. But Abbie and her friends knew it was no love for his babe that actuated him, and that they must again live in constant fear of molestation.

And they were not mistaken. Hardly three days at a time passed in which he did not call to see his "darling babe." On such occasions he kept up a constant grumbling about the treatment the child received. Either she was not dressed warm enough, or she was togged up too much, or he did not believe she was properly fed, and he ought to be allowed to come in and take care of her—his precious, abused baby—always ending by wishing he had not brought her back.

Thus was Abbie's life made as miserable as it was in his power to make it.

CHAPTER XXII.

THE CASE FINALLY DECIDED IN ABBIE'S FAVOR.

ONE day in March, after Abbie had returned home, Steve called and seemed to be very sad. As he took the babe in his arms, he begged to be allowed to step into Deering's a few minutes with her, saying he would take the bottle of milk along and take good care of her, and promising to bring her back in an hour.

"Oh, I dare not let her go!" cried Abbie in alarm.

"But why not?" asked he. "You know I dare not break my word, and I will surely bring her back."

Without waiting for an answer, he moved swiftly away.

Abbie was much frightened at this, and, running out, she informed her brothers, who were at work in the barn, what had occurred. A strict watch was kept, and in about an hour he was seen to leave the house, but instead of returning to her, as he had promised to do, he started toward the village with the babe in his arms. An alarm was instantly given, though as secretly as possible. Soon he was seen to enter the deserted house where Abbie had spent

(284)

so many unhappy hours, which was now empty. Here there was no means of building a fire.

For three hours he remaimed here, often going to the door, from which he could be seen from Mr. Saunders', and tossing the babe up and down to try to attract attention. He had no idea that he was being watched, but enjoyed the thought that they dare not attack him. In this he was in one sense right, for they feared for the babe, and did not mean to attack him if it could be avoided.

At last Ella grew indignant at such nursing, and began to cry lustily. This made it more unpleasant for both parties, and just as the boys were about to enter at one door, he passed out at the other and walked swiftly toward the house. Seeing Abbie waiting at the gate he turned abruptly and entered Mr. Deering's, where he left the child and passed out at the other door.

Raz had not been far behind, and quickly followed him into the house. Mrs. Deering gladly gave him the babe, and it was soon safe in its mother's arms. But Raz was not quick enough but what Steve, who had again entered the house, saw him, and his anger knew no bounds. Running at full speed, he was soon at the house.

But as he attempted to force an entrance, Raz met him, and, presenting a pistol, fired. But Steve, springing quickly to one side, avoided the shot, then, springing to the middle of the road, he stopped, and, opening his vest, while he struck a tragic attitude, dared him to fire.

Raz coolly replied that he did not shoot men on the public highway. Then, saying that the contract with Abbie was broken, that she would see him no more, and that any attempt on his part to enter the premises would be considered trespass, and punished as such, he entered and closed the door behind him.

Steve was struck dumb at this announcement. He saw that he had again overshot his mark, and that Raz was in earnest, and he felt convinced that his persecution must cease. He could not mistake the meaning of either the words or manner of Raz, and turning he walked hurriedly away.

Abbie had heard the words of her brother, and she felt that he would stand by her. She had determined in her heart that this should break off her agreement with her tormentor, and she felt truly thankful that Raz was so prompt to proclaim her freedom. When he entered the room, she was weeping softly on her baby's neck.

"Why, sister mine, what does this mean?" said he. "I think you ought to be laughing instead of weeping like that. Don't you know this is the best day's work we have done? Don't you see he has broken his agreement, and you are free?"

"Yes," said she, "and my tears this time are tears of joy, partly that I am free at last, but more that I have such a brave and loving brother."

"I thank you for the compliment, sister mine, though I don't see much to praise. I would have been a coward indeed to show fear at such a time.

And as for the rest, how could I help it, with such a sister, and such a mother?" and the young man looked fondly at his mother, whose eyes were full of tears, while a holy peace seemed to light up her face.

She had heard the conversation of her children, and her heart was raised in thankfulness to heaven for the love that existed between them.

Abbie's eyes followed those of her brother, and she felt the truth of his words. How indeed could they prove untrue to the instincts of love and truth with such a mother!

Mingled with the feeling of joy and love in the heart of the mother was one of gratitude to her Heavenly Father that her son was not a murderer. No pen can describe the fear and anguish in that mother's heart as she saw the weapon in the hands of her son, pointed, as it seemed to her, with unerring aim at the head of the intruder. But so sudden had been the movement that she had no time for more than a silent prayer ere the danger was past, and her heart rose to God in praise that his hands were still unstained with blood.

Something of the same feeling found its place in the heart of the brother and sister, and who shall say that the mother's unspoken prayer did not receive its answer.

All this had passed in much less time than it takes to tell it, and Andy and Will did not reach the house until Steve was leaving it. They soon heard all there was to tell, and all agreed that the contract had been rendered null and void by this act of Steve's. Yet they did not believe he would acknowledge this, and Raz proposed that, as the court would not meet until the twenty-fifth of April, Abbie should be secretly conveyed to some safe retreat, where her presence would remain unknown to her enemy, and thus she would escape further annoyance.

She tremblingly accepted the proposition. The only thing that remained to be done was to fix upon the proper place and manner of conveying her there. Raz had his plans well laid, but it was decided to wait until the father's return before settling their plans.

Mr. Saunders returned, and was informed of the occurrence of the day. He was greatly troubled. The anxiety of the last few months had told upon him, and he knew not what to do. When, therefore, Raz laid his proposition before him, he grasped it eagerly, wondering that he had not thought of it before.

"I know just the place for her," he said, his face lighting up with animation.

"Where?" asked two or three at once.

"You know where I went this winter for provisions."

"High Forest," said Raz quickly.

"The same. Well, I got my provisions of an old farmer by the name of Hill. I have often spoken of him."

"Yes, 1 know," said Raz, impatiently waiting for more.

"1 have seldom formed the acquaintance of a man I would as willingly trust as Mr. Hill. I believe our regard is mutual, and that he would as gladly do me a good turn as I would him. I was thinking of going there to-morrow for fresh supplies, and could take Abbie along, and, if all was agreeable, leave her there. No one in these parts knows of my acquaintance in that place, and she will be perfectly safe."

This plan met the approval of all concerned. It was decided that they would start at two the next morning, Anda volunteering to accompany them to guard against surprise, while Will and Raz remained at home to lull suspicion, and, if possible, hide the fact of her departure till the return of Mr. Saunders.

This settled, Anda returned home to acquaint his wife with the plan and prepare for his journey. Abbie at once set about preparations, while conflicting emotions filled her heart. She felt that the decision was a wise one and willingly acquiesced, yet she dreaded the night journey, the exposure to her babe, and, in spite of her father's faith in the willingness of his new friend to receive her, she dreaded coming thus unexpectedly upon them with the request. She had felt so keenly the anxiety and care that had come upon her friends for her sake, and she began to look upon herself as a bur-

19

den, and doubted that strangers would be willing to take upon themselves the responsibility of her presence. Instinctively her heart went up to God for support and strength, and straight from the presence of her Heavenly Father seemed to come the all-sufficient answer, "Trust in me, my child." Never had the blessed words sounded sweeter to her ears than at this moment. Looking up toward heaven, she cried fervently, "O God, I thank thee that I have a God in whom I can trust." She retired that night with more of love and trust than fear and dread in her heart.

She was aroused at one by her mother, and, after a hasty toilet, went to her parents in the kitchen, where a warm meal had been prepared, and where they were soon joined by Anda and Mr. Thomas, who had volunteered to accompany them.

They had just finished the midnight meal when Will and Raz announced that the team was waiting. With many sweet words of encouragement from her mother, she bade her a tearful good-by, and they were soon on the road.

It was a cold, dark night, lighted only by the faint glimmer of the stars, and as Abbie took her seat in the sleigh and was closely tucked in with blankets, a terrible sense of loneliness came over her; tears sprang to her eyes, and a choking sensation nearly stopped her breath.

"When will this weary wandering cease, and I be allowed to rest?" she cried. Bowing her head

over her babe, she allowed the tears to flow for a
time unchecked. None would ever know the bitter pain it had cost her to consent thus to throw
herself upon the hospitality of strangers, or how
strongly tempted she had been to beg her parents
to let her remain with them. Her objections had
been checked at first by sympathy for them, then
her judgment told her that the plan was a good
one, yet there had been such a longing to remain
with her friends, and such a dread of strangers and
trusting her safety with them, that it was with difficulty that she could hide her feelings from them.

When morning made its appearance, it found our
heroine in a more calm state of mind. With a determined effort she had succeeded in putting her
feelings aside, and appearing quite cheerful during
the hours of preparation for her journey. Not till
she was snugly tucked in among the robes, and
fairly out into the night, with the curtain of darkness around her, did she give way to her feelings.
Then she wept bitterly for a time, wept from
mingled exhaustion and dread of what was still to
come. It seemed hard that she, who had always
tried to have her ways governed by the Bible rules
of right and wrong, should be called to suffer so;
that while others, who seemed governed only by
their own sweet wills, were the possessors of sweet
homes and kind husbands, she must go out into
the strange world, among strange faces, and in
strange places, to seek the protection of a hidden

home. How hard it seemed, and how bitter the tears she shed!

At first her thoughts were entirely of herself, and full of pity for herself, that she must bear so hard a lot. But soon she began to notice her surroundings. They were out on the bleak, snow-covered prairie, with no habitation of man in sight. The wind blew in fierce gusts, often whirling the snow in their faces, and in the bitter cold the fine particles seemed like needles.

As she noticed all this, the feeling of loneliness increased, almost to desperation. Just then her father, who sat on the seat in front of her, groaned aloud, as he shifted in his seat, apparently to find an easy position.

The sound smote her to the heart. Poor, dear old father! How much he was suffering and enduring for her sake! How feeble and worn he looked! Her heart warmed with love for him, he who ought to be safe in bed this bitter night. Then her thoughts flew back over the last four months. She thought of the many nights of broken rest, of the many journeys through the bitter cold he had endured for her. How kind and loving he had been to her all this time, never seeming to think of himself or the trouble she caused him, but ever pitying her for her sufferings!

Then away flew her busy mind back to the years of her childhood, with her father's form continually before her. She remembered how she had been

led to accept Christ as her Saviour through his
kind teaching, when only ten years of age; how she
had tried to do her duty in the fear of God ever
since, and then, as she thought of her present situation, a something akin to rebellion began to creep
into her heart.

But her thoughts did not rest here. They seemed
determined to make her see herself and her past
life as she had never seen it before. She remembered how happy she had been when Steve Rushford first came to her father's house.

She thought of her former lover, and of her refusal of him without the advice of her parents, although she well knew he was approved of them;
then of her acceptance of this man in the same
way, leaving her parents to consent or force her to
break her word. She thought of that earnest talk
with her father when his consent was asked. He
had tried to persuade her to wait for one year, but
she had refused even this.

Had she been actuated by the right spirit in those
days? Had she been seeking divine aid and walking in the fear of God? Her heart seemed to cease
beating as she asked herself these questions. She
could but answer, No. For the first time in all
these weary months she began to see that her trouble
had been brought about by her own acts. Had
she shown a disposition to listen to her father's advice, she felt sure he would have saved her from all
this trouble. She had not meant to be ungrateful

or disobedient, but she now saw that she had been
both.   Yet as she looked back over the last few
months, she remembered that she had received
nothing but kindness at his hands.   Not once had
he reproached her for her disobedience.   Though
bowed down with grief, he had ever been kind and
tender with her.

As she thought of these things, her heart seemed
filled with a strange commotion.   The thought of
the unwavering tenderness of her earthly father
brought thoughts of the goodness of her heavenly
Father, who, though she had sinned, had not forsaken her, but had delivered her from her persecu-
tor—for such she now considered him whom, in
girlish ignorance, see had promised to love, honor,
and obey.

She felt thankful that, in looking back over her
life with Rushford, she could find nothing to reproach herself with.   She had faithfully tried to do
her duty by him, and had tried with all her might
to avert the trouble which came at last.   She had
been convinced for some time before their separation
that he not only did not love her, but that he was
growing tired of the quiet life he was forced to live.

As these thoughts crowded through her mind,
the babe in her arms stirred uneasily, and her
thoughts at once turned toward it.   Her feelings
had been softened and subdued by the thoughts she
had indulged, and now an overwhelming sense of
the goodness of God in bringing her through all

her troubles, even to returning her babe safely to her arms, came over her.

Her feelings were fairly transformed. The very journey she was now making, which a few moments before seemed such a trial, she was willing now to accept as a blessing, for was it not to bear her, with her precious babe, to a haven of safety? In this new light how foolish seemed her former repinings! The more she thought of it, the more ungrateful it seemed.

With an earnest prayer for forgiveness for past sins, and for strength to live a different life, she determined to spend no more time in fruitless repinings, but to accept the blessings that came to her lot and make the most of them.

When morning came, it found her in a more hopeful state of mind than she had been in since her trouble began. After a short halt to feed their teams, they passed on, and two o'clock P. M. found them at their destination.

As they drew up at the door of the farmhouse, Mr. Hill came out to meet them. He was a tall, heavily-built man, with a ruddy face and a kindly smile, and he gave them such a hearty welcome that it sent a thrill of pleasure through Abbie's heart. All feelings of dread left her. When he ushered them into the large, old-fashioned kitchen, and she met Mrs. Hill, she felt that they were indeed friends.

The noon meal, which had been delayed on ac-

count of the absence of some of the family, was
announced.   As they gathered about the table,
the warmest seats were reserved for their guests.
After all were served, the conversation became gen-
eral, and Abbie had time to scan the faces before
her.   At the head of the table sat the farmer; at his
right sat his daughter, a girl of twelve, with a bright,
independent air, showing that she appreciated the
position of only daughter; and knew how to make
the most of it.   At his left sat Wallace, the oldest
son, who was a little under the medium size, with
a quiet manner, while the expression of his eyes
and mouth showed him to be firm as well as kind.
Next sat Marion.   He was tall, strongly built like
his father; he had light blue eyes, a smiling face,
and seemed to be running over with fun; it was
easy to see he was loved by all, and adored by the
little ones.   Abbie felt that she had indeed fallen
into good hands, and no longer wondered at her
father's choice of a place of hiding for her.   The
evening passed pleasantly away, and when, in the
morning, Abbie saw her father drive away, it was
with less of regret than she would have thought
possible twenty-four hours before.

Abbie had requested that she might be allowed
to assist in the household duties, feeling that she
could better endure the hours of waiting.   Her
friends had kindly given their consent, so, as soon
as her father had disappeared from sight, she returned to the kitchen, went resolutely to work, and,

as the hours of the day passed pleasantly away, she was surprised at the feeling of rest and quiet that settled down upon her, and ere she retired to rest, she put up a prayer of thanksgiving to her Father in heaven, who she knew was watching over her for good, and then slept as she had not slept for many a night. The next day, and for several days, the weather continued fine, but the 20th of March a terrible storm set in, the snow falling thick and fast, the wind blowing fiercely, piling the snow in drifts in the fence corners and filling the hollows in some places twenty feet deep. It raged as only a western blizzard can, making man and beast appreciate shelter and food for several days; then it cleared away, leaving the air clear and cold, but soon changing to milder weather, showing signs of a thaw. All were glad of the change, for they were getting tired of winter, and knew that the fields would soon be green again.

None but those who have spent a winter on the broad prairies of Minnesota, or a similar place, can ever realize the thrill of pleasure, accompanied by renewed vigor, that fills the whole. being of man, woman, and child, as, by one sign after another, they mark the sure change from winter, with all its terrors, to spring, with its sweet, balmy air, which transforms the snow-clad earth to a garden with greensward and springing flowers.

Abbie and her new-found friends were not unconscious of its influence. So kind were Abbie's friends, and so peaceful were the days, that life seemed brighter than she had dared to hope it would be, and hope began once more to spring up in her heart.

Little Ella had lost that pinched, pitiful look which had touched the heart of everyone who saw her on her return, and was growing fat and plump. As Abbie felt the dear baby arms clasped about her neck, her heart swelled with gratitude to Him who had preserved her precious one and returned her safe to her arms. Each day she strove to consecrate herself anew to His service. She no longer felt to murmur at her lot, but strove in every way to prove her appreciation of the kindness bestowed upon her by these new friends.

At last the long-looked-for day had come and passed. A letter was received bearing the precious news of her freedom, and that, on a certain date, her friends would come for her. Mingled with the feeling of joy at the prospect of again being at home was that of sadness at parting with those who, in time of need, had proved themselves to be friends indeed.

And when, one beautiful morning in April, she took leave of the farmer's family and set out for home, she felt that she was leaving friends behind her. As she neared home she felt some misgivings lest new trials should await her, but these fears were groundless, for Rushford had given up the contest, and she never saw him again.

In time she came to feel more secure and even happy. A few years after, she married a gentleman who proved to be a tender and loving husband, and a kind and indulgent father to Ella.

Abbie is now the mother of a large family of sons and daughters, who are at once her pride and joy. But all her days of joy or sorrow are softened by the memory of those days of trial and final triumph, and the precious lessons of faith and trust taught her by her mother.

Here my story ends. If the perusal of this little volume shall cause one maiden who is inclined to take the vows of matrimony upon herself without due consideration, to pause and think ere it is too late, and thus escape a similar fate, the writer will feel amply repaid for her labor.